Mary Clemmer

Poems of Life and Nature

Mary Clemmer

Poems of Life and Nature

ISBN/EAN: 9783337408350

Printed in Europe, USA, Canada, Australia, Japan

Cover: Foto ©Andreas Hilbeck / pixelio.de

More available books at **www.hansebooks.com**

POEMS

OF

LIFE AND NATURE

BY

MARY CLEMMER

BOSTON

JAMES R. OSGOOD AND COMPANY

1883

UNIVERSITY PRESS:
JOHN WILSON AND SON, CAMBRIDGE.

Dedicated

TO

MY DEAREST FRIEND.

CONTENTS.

Life.

	PAGE
LIFE–THREADS	17
THE DAYS	20
CHANGE	24
A FEW MORE MORNINGS	29
SOMETHING BEYOND	32
THE YESTERDAYS	34
TO-MORROW	36
MY WIFE AND I	38
WHEN BABY COMES	41
THE CHILDLESS MOTHER	44
THE LOST PET	46
THE LITTLE BOOT	51
NOT DEAD	55
VANISHED FACES	59
FOREVER LIVES THE KING	61
IN MEMORY	63

PAGE

One Bond 65

The Guest 66

On the Ferry 69

The Sunset 72

Sleep 74

Rest 76

Waste 77

Discord 79

Reproof 82

Silence 83

Loss 85

Knowledge 86

The Yachts 88

By the Sea 90

Room 92

I might have done 94

Two Angels 96

One Death 99

Valery 102

The Good Angel 106

My Place 110

Idle 114

Last Roses 118

The Hermit-Thrush 121

The Doves 123

Fall in 127

A Ballad of the Border 130

The Journalist 137

Love.

	PAGE
WORDS FOR PARTING	145
GOOD-BY, SWEETHEART	147
PRESENCE	149
SONG	153
GOOD-NIGHT	154
FAREWELL	157
INJUNCTION	159
INTERROGATION	161

Nature.

THANKSGIVING	165
ARBUTUS	167
THE SEED	172
A PERFECT DAY	175
THE MOUNTAIN PINE	177
AN OCTOBER IDYL	184
GOLDEN-ROD	186
NANTASKET	191
AN OCTOBER PICTURE	196
HAPPY DAYS	200

Religion

ALONE WITH GOD	205
A WOMAN'S HYMN TO CHRIST	208
WAITING	211

PAGE

SABBATH VERSES 213

REST 216

AN OUTCAST 219

THE CHRISTMAS CHRIST 223

LOSS AND GAIN 228

QUESTIONS 229

LIGHT 233

TO AN INFIDEL 236

GO NOT AWAY 240

A LITANY 242

A CONVERSATION 244

THE CHRIST 249

PRAY THOU FOR ME 252

THE MESSAGE 254

Sonnets.

TO RALPH WALDO EMERSON 259

TO JOHN GREENLEAF WHITTIER, I. 260

TO JOHN GREENLEAF WHITTIER, II. 261

APHRODITE URANIA 262

HERA 263

PALLAS ATHENA 264

A MAGNOLIA GRANDIFLORA 265

FRUITAGE 266

INADEQUACY 267

FATE 268

RENUNCIATION 269

	PAGE
OPULENCE	270
SECRETIVENESS	271
DISTANCE	272
RECOGNITION	273
THE FRIEND	274
THE LOVER	275
FULFILMENT	276
THE CATHEDRAL PINES, I.	277
THE CATHEDRAL PINES, II.	278
THE JOY OF WORK	279

LIFE.

LIFE.

———◦❖◦———

LIFE-THREADS.

OUT of life's tangled skein
    Draw here and there a thread;
And one is black with pain,
  And one with grief is red,
  To show a heart hath bled.

And one is white as youth;
  It marks its perfect time,
When life, untouched of ruth,
  Mounted toward Summer prime,
  Through love, romance, and rhyme.

Beside Love's glowing threads,
  Here one is cool and gray,
Where passionate morning weds
  A neutral-tinted day,
  And Peace comes down to stay.

2

Imperial purple this,
　　To tyrannize and prey,
With hint of loftier bliss
　　Set in its royal ray,
　　Yet calm to hurt or slay.

Pallid and paling lines
　　Of youth forever fled.
Signs!   They are only signs
　　Of the living joy long dead, —
　　Wraiths for the eyes bespread.

Yet, touching them, they glow, —
　　Again the young, warm thrill,
The tones all sweet and low,
　　The hushed heart waiting still,
　　As eyes with love o'erfill.

Memory her trophy yields
　　To the Present's happier real;
We pace the Summer fields,
　　We move to Hope's ideal,
　　And Faith and Love are leal.

We seat us down some day;
　And from life's tangled skein,
That Memory holds alway,
　We smooth out lines of pain,
　And love-threads hold pure gain.

O myriad-tinted threads!
　We gather you all at last;
You mark our whitening heads,
　You bind us to our past,
　And we hold you close and fast.

THE DAYS.

THE days, the days, the swift, mute days
    That fly across our fitful ways,
That bear us through the tangled maze
We call our life, — the days! the days!

I fain would hold them back betimes;
I would not haste to reach the climes
Whose glad inhabitants ne'er say,
"To-day, mine own, — O dear to-day!"

I sigh not for the heavenly ways
That wait above our checkered days;
I love these days that fly so fast, —
These mortal days that cannot last.

'T is made of days, our meagre span,
In links that bind for bliss or ban;
They fold us in their shadows dun,
They bear the splendors of the sun.

They bar our life, the chill, void days
That give us naught, — the day that preys
And eats our heart, while slow we smile
Upon the crowd, with piteous guile.

I dread thee in the dawning gray,
As slow the long night wanes away,
O dark to-day, O dire to-day,
That smites so low, and smites to slay.

In memory they gloom and shine,
Life's symbols sad, — the red-rose sign
Of Love's own day; a leaf or line
Tells where it filled or spilled its wine.

We bind them slowly in our sheaves,
The day that robs, the day that grieves;
Slow-moving on, we cry, " Forget,
Forsake the dark land of regret."

Then, on the gardens of our slain,
A light of joy — untouched of pain,
Serene with promise — slow doth shine,
Light from a later day divine.

The Indian Summer of the heart,
Its breath of balm heals bitterest smart;
From buried Summer's passionate heat
Are born its blossoms pure and sweet.

Heart, gather in thine aftermath;
What far, faint fragrances it hath!
What calm broods down the storm-swept way!
What beauty veins the fair, meek day!

What music murmurs fine and clear!
What peace pervades its atmosphere!
What love, what dear companionships,
Pour from the eyes, the voice, the lips!

What courage, what high patience sweet,
What rest, what tenderness complete, —
What trust in God, what faith in man,
In woman, meet in one day's span!

The noontide of thy perfect beam
Must faint and fail, O day supreme, —
Thy bliss die out of mortal skies,
To dawn far on in Paradise.

Thou day of days!   Thy pulses run
Into my life, and we are one;
Far on in deep content I'll say,
"My life began that day, *that* day."

CHANGE.

WE lay our dear ones in earth's prisoning
      mould,
And, when we see the grasses growing green
Between us and the faces that we love,
We call it sorrow. Call it sorrow, though
The ministering months do tend our sleepers well.
Mellifluous Spring, through tender-throated leaves,
Rains down her melodies to lull their rest;
And Summer, mid her carnival of bloom,
Drops tears of dew upon their tired heads.
And Autumn, all forgetting to be sear,
More pied with splendor than the bowery June,
Doth bind her jewels on each low-laid brow;
While beryl-leaves, bossed on her blazoned vest,
Are crimson-stained, as if her heart had bled,
And grief's red wound to all the world lay bare.

Then Winter softly in her hooded snows
Folds every darling.   Comfortless we grieve
When earth takes back into her gentle arms
Her weary children, when the loving Christ
Folds on his bosom souls he died for once.
When, far from this world's bitter blight and cold,
Our lambs are taken, evermore to roam
In fairer pastures in the upper fold,
'T is not life's saddest sorrow; albeit we cry,
And blame the Shepherd that he loved his own.

To be life's soul and beauty unto one;
To fill the measure of one being's need,
Till all love's light and joyance flows from you, —
The might to do life's work, to bear life's ill,
Springing from inspiration in your eyes,
And from the " God-speed " of your loving voice,
Low-tuned to tremulous tenderness; to be
The soul of life and loveliness to one,
That Change may come and build a wall between
You and your idol, — looking down on you
With calm, cold, cruel eyes, with taunting tone,
Slow-uttering in the silence, o'er and o'er:
" Your love will never need you any more,

Nor ever, *ever* need you any more,"——
This is the saddest thing in life to me.

I read one day ('t was in a quaint, old book)
That every friendship, like an ancient glove,
Doth grow ungainly, waxing loose at last,
And finally wears out.   We fling it by,
And flaunt a newer, suiting newer need.
So shall I pull the drawer of memory out?
And toss old names about, — as oft old gloves,
All moiled and marred, with gaping rent distraught,
Yet sweet with lavender, whose tang they stole
In lush May morns, to make caressing airs
Full fraught with fragrance when they went with
      me?
Shall I forgetful — aye, ungrateful — say,
With scornful touch and toss: " O yes, old gloves,
You 're soiled, you 're all worn out; yet sooth I fain
Would find a pair among you, cast away,
To suit my need upon a rainy day "?
Thus search your names for sordid use, O friends!
Thus like a garment seared, sore-worn, tossed by,
I fling you up and down my careless way?
Ah, nay!   I hold you most religiously,

I count your names a rosary in my prayers;
Nor separation, with its saddest change,
Can change for me the faces that I love.
The twilight purples stain the leaning hills;
The fusing seas of primrose light beyond
Hide all the Eden that lies *still beyond;*
But tides of memory are setting in,
And flowing downward through the sunset gates,
All freighted o'er with treasure.   Lo! I see
Face after face float in the water calm;
A knot of faded flowers — a souvenir
Of one lost day, serene in peace — drifts by;
A ripple of soft sound breaks through the waves,
The lingering echo of beloved speech;
The cadence low of most melodious song
Thrills through the silence of the past to me.
O absent, unforgotten!   If mine once,
Mine always.   Though no real, sighed-for tone
Pierces the stillness; though I sit alone,
And, leaning back, glean every helpful word
And scattered joy that I dropped yesterday;
And though I'm fain to fill the gloaming void
With loving memories of your dear eyes;
Though never any more, day after day,

Your smile's soft sunshine may light all my soul,
Your words ring joyful welcomes when I come;
Though Time may rob me, till 't will die at last,
Love's golden iterance, "We love you, — ay,
We need you always," — shall I sadly cry:
"The love I lived for hath slipped far from me, —
Because it is not, it hath never been?"
Nay! — still I 'll count you sacredly my own:
Not mine to hold through lure of voice or eye,
Nor spell of presence, nor the quick, sweet thrill
Of eager-meeting, slow-receding hands,
Nor precious seal of holy lip on lip;
Not mine to have, to bless, to lean on long;
Yet through the everlasting years my own,
To love, to pray for, and to live for still!
I lift each name into the oriflamme
Of God's own love, and say: "Lord, love my
  friends,
And let me love them in thy purer world!"

A FEW MORE MORNINGS.

A FEW more mornings, yet a few more mornings,
  We'll watch the light's low dawning, dull and
    gray;
A few more mornings, and we'll faintly murmur
  To those who love us, "'T is our latest day."
From weary brows will fall the life-worn mask,
From tired hands will drop the half-done task.

A few more mornings, but a few more mornings,
  Others will take the work that we laid down, —
Will lift it where we left it in the shadows,
  Will bear its cross, perchance will wear the crown
We sighed for, toiled for, all our fleeting hours, —
The crown of crowns, that never could be ours.

A few more mornings!   Amid distant dawnings,
 They who come after us will softly say:
"Where now the labor of those gone before us,
 The recompense of all their burdened day?
They are not missed where they were always seen,
All life moves on as if they had not been."

A few more mornings!   Still will be forever
 The heart that thrills to-day with love's dear
  pain.
Its suffering done, all done the long endeavor,
 The far-out yearning of the lofty brain, —
There 'll be in the low house where we lie down
No love, no hate, no dream of high renown.

A few more morns!   'T will all be told, our story,
 So sweet, so brief.   Why war with changeless
  fate?
Why cry for love?   Why spend our strength for
  glory?
 Why pray to God with prayer importunate?
His centuries go; we still must come and pass
But as the shadows on the Summer grass.

A few more mornings, — then again in beauty
  The earth will wear the splendor of her springs;
While we, within the universe of spirits,
  Will wander somewhere among viewless things.
Where'er it be, in all the heaven of air,
We still must see our human home is fair;
Wondrous must be God's gift to compensate
For all we miss within our human fate.

SOMETHING BEYOND.

SOMETHING beyond!   Though now, with joy
        unfound,
  The life-task falleth from thy weary hand,
Be brave, be patient!   In the fair Beyond
        Thou 'lt understand.

Thou 'lt understand why our most royal hours
  Couch sorrowful slaves, bound by low nature's
        greed, —
Why the celestial soul 's a minion made
        To narrowest need.

In this pent sphere of being incomplete —
  The imperfect fragment of a beauteous whole —
For yon rare regions, where the perfect meet,
        Sighs the lone soul. —

Sighs for the perfect!   Far and fair it lies;
   It hath no half-fed friendships perishing fleet,
No partial insight, no averted eyes,
     No loves unmeet.

Something beyond!   Light for our clouded eyes!
   In this dark dwelling, in its shrouded beams,
Our Best waits masked; few pierce the soul's
     disguise;
     How sad it seems!

Something beyond!   Ah, if it were not so,
   Darker would be thy face, O brief To-day!
Earthward we 'd bow beneath life's smiting woe,
     Powerless to pray.

Something beyond!   The immortal morning stands
   Above the night, clear shines her prescient
     brow;
The pendulous star in her transfigured hands
     Lights up the Now.

THE YESTERDAYS.

I TAKE your gifts, O Yesterdays,
   And, safe from all unfriendly eyes,
I set them one by one away,
   Secure from change or sore surprise.

I take your gifts, glad Yesterday;
   And when I turn from work to play,
From care to rest, they'll make my joy,
   And give my heart its holiday.

I take your gifts, sad Yesterday —
   The better deeds I might have done,
The tears I might have wiped away,
   The higher heights I might have won.

You show, O tearful Yesterdays,
    How poor my life's most perfect part;
You tear the crown of pride away,
    And give instead the pitying heart.

I see the wave of Summer woods,
    I hear the lapse of far-off streams;
The murmur of the honeyed pines
    Runs sweet and low along my dreams.

And still a tender heart enfolds
    A faded face, a haunting tone —
The lingering fragrance of a joy,
    One Yesterday made all its own.

I take your griefs, rich Yesterdays!
    Henceforth may no soul call me poor;
Fortune may strip her gauds away,
    The wealth of all the past is sure.

We jostle in the careless crowd, —
    We meet, we part, we go our ways;
But each, unseen, bears up to God
    The sum of all his Yesterdays.

TO - MORROW.

A SHINING isle in a stormy sea,
　　We seek it ever with smiles and sighs;
To-day is sad.　In the bland To-be,
　　Serene and lovely To-morrow lies.

It mocked us, the beautiful Yesterday;
　　It left us poorer.　Oh, never mind!
In the fair To-morrow, far away,
　　It waits the joy that we failed to find.

"With fitful labor and meagre gain,
　　Life is a failure."　Be still my heart!
To-day — the partial result, the pain;
　　To-morrow — fruition, the perfect part.

Time looks from our eyes with tenderest ruth,
　It touches with silver the locks of gold;
It kisses away the tints of youth,
　Till we say, " To-morrow we shall be old."

We think of the countries far and fair,
　All free forever from blight and frost;
Where love lives on in the holy air,
　We 'll find again the youth we had lost.

'T will still go on — the belovèd task,
　That drops half done from thy weary hand —
Thy crown for another! " Why?" you ask.
　Thou 'lt waken To-morrow, and understand.

Nothing is finished.　From birth to the pall —
　Our love, our sorrow, life's dear, brief day —
Is a little fragment, that is all,
　Of the *more* that wait in the Far-away.

Why we are sorry, we shall divine,
　When the life that is perfect holds its sway, —
When peace abides in the Thine and Mine,
　And To-morrow melts into God's To-day.

MY WIFE AND I.

WE 'RE drifting out to isles of peace;
    We let the weary world go by;
We sail away o'er Summer seas,
    My wife and I.

We bear to rest in regions fair
    The faltering spirit of the mind;
The kingdom wide, of toil and care,
    We leave behind.

How poor to us the proudest prize
    For which earth's weary millions sigh;
Our meed we see in two dear eyes,
    My wife and I.

This way and that the races go,
　　All seeking some way to be blest;
Nor dream the joy they never know
　　　　Is how to rest.

The travailing nations rise and fall,
　　They lift the palm, they bear the rue;
Yet bliss is this, — to know, through all,
　　　　That one is true.

They perish swift, the gala flowers
　　The lauding people love to fling;
Waits silence, dearth, and lonely hours,
　　　　The once-crowned king.

But never shall he faint or fall
　　Who lists to hear, o'er every fate,
The sweeter and the higher call
　　　　Of his true mate.

I hear it wheresoe'er I rove;
　　She holds me safe from shame or sin;
The holy temple of her love
　　　　I worship in.

We 're drifting out to realms of peace;
　We let the weary world go by;
We sail away o'er Summer seas,
　　My wife and I.

We sail to regions calm and still, —
　To bring in time, to all behind,
The service of exalted will,
　　Of tranquil mind.

The fading shores grow far and dim,
　The stars are lighting in the sky;
We sail away to Ocean's hymn,
　　My wife and I.

WHEN BABY COMES.

WHAT a hush is in the house!
  Charley, lonesome little mouse,
Round his nursery must roam,
Tearful alien in his home,
  Now Baby 's come.

"Charley's nose is out of joint,"
Sad his Aunties say, and point
To the doleful little man,
Headman of the growing clan,
  Now Baby 's come.

All the world has gone awry
To Charley's heart. None heed his cry,
Potent law until to-day.
Charley calls, but none obey,
  For Baby 's come.

"Go!" he cries; "Take *her* away!
I don't like her.   She can't play."
Quivering grief and tearful joy:
" *Charley, he* is Mamma's boy!
          Take *her* away."

Wondrous fair!   The pillowing lace
Frames the lovely mother's face.
Ah! her heart can hold the two,
Eyes of brown and eyes of blue,
          When Baby comes.

Baby brings all love along,
Ever growing, ever strong;
Soundless wells of tenderness,
Never ebb nor grow the less
          When Baby comes.

What a hint of faint perfume,
What a hush is in the room!
All the loud world put to rout,
All its vanity shut out,
          When Baby comes.

'T is a temple; on its shrine
Trembles everything divine
Unto one. *His* Heaven lies
In the spheres of her soft eyes,
    When Baby comes.

Far the wild world's fret and snare,
Endless business, weary care;
Once again romance is sweet,
Life is young and love complete,
    When Baby comes.

All the earth is made anew, —
Far the false, and fair the true, —
Where a little life begins,
Free of sorrow, free of sins,
    And Baby comes.

THE CHILDLESS MOTHER.

I LAY my tasks down one by one;
   I sit in the silence in twilight's grace.
Out of the shadows, deep and dun,
   Steals, like a star, my Baby's face.

How mocking cold are the world's poor joys!
   How poor to me all its pomp and pride!
In my lap lie the Baby's idle toys;
   In this very room the Baby died.

I will shut these broken toys away
   Under the lid, where they mutely bide.
I will smile in the face of noisy day,
   Just as if Baby had never died.

I will take up my work once more,
　As if I had never laid it down.
Who will dream that I ever wore,
　In triumph, motherhood's sacred crown?

Who will deem my life ever bore
　Fruit, the sweeter in grief and pain?
The flitting smile that the Baby wore
　Outrayed the light of the loftiest brain.

I shall meet him, in the world's rude din,
　Who hath outlived his mother's kiss, —
Who hath forsaken her love, for sin!
　I shall be spared her pang in this.

Man's way is hard, and sore beset;
　Many may fall, but few can win.
Thanks, dear Shepherd! my lamb is safe, —
　Safe from sorrow, and safe from sin.

Nevertheless, the way is long,
　And tears leap up in the light of the sun.
I 'd give my world for a cradle-song,
　And a kiss from Baby — only one.

THE LOST PET.

OH, where 's my pet, my pet?
  I dream I see her yet,
Playing beside me on the mossy floor;
I turn to find her, but the play is o'er, —
  Alas, the play is o'er!

Oh, where 's my pet, my pet?
  My eyes are all unwet,
Dried by the fever of my long despair;
My empty hands ache for their wonted care,
  The child that made life fair.

Where are the carolling feet,
  Playing with music sweet,
Playing beside me on the parlor floor?
Their music dies on the far spirit-shore,
  Their music 's mine no more.

And still I will forget,
And wait their coming yet;
Her playthings lie here scattered all about,
As if a moment, mid the merry rout,
My darling had slipped out.

In perfumed drawer I lay
Her treasures all away —
These little shoes, this gay embroidered dress;
In these silk flowers I wrought my tenderness,
My yearning need to bless.

Ah, never rioting boys
Shall break these pretty toys,
My sweet girl-baby played with long before!
Here from all eyes I hide my hoarded store,
No child shall use them more.

My pet, I see thee yet!
Thine eyes of liquid jet,
Untraced by grief or life's hard history,
Brimful of mystery, a prophecy
Of riper bliss to be!

Then only this, I knew,
Shone starlike through their dew —
The morning love-light of a dawning soul,
The woman-love, her guerdon and her goal,
Her being, bale, and dole.

Oh, was it from some snare,
Some slow and sure despair,
Some soundless sorrow never to be told,
The pitying Christ bore to his upper fold,
My lamb from out the cold?

Still, in my weak despair,
Through the vast voids of air,
My sick soul calls thee with a voice forlorn;
I bleed for the young life from my life torn,
The love from my love shorn.

I want the warm child-lips,
The rosy finger-tips,
Nestling in mine once more at twilight fall, —
Listening to hear the quick step in the hall,
To hear the evening call

Of the belovèd voice,
Which made our hearts rejoice.
I yearn to see the twinkling little feet,
All tremulously eager, fly to greet
Papa, with kisses sweet.

The joy is over now;
Bind poppies on my brow,
Numb all my senses, that I may not know
My baby lies below the winter snow;
O God, that it is so!

The long unbroken gloom,
The silence of this room,
How can I bear it as the days move on, —
As years creep on how can I live alone,
Shorn of my beautiful one?

They tell me I'll forget,
Will cease to need thee yet,
While other children round my hearth shall play —
When later joys are born, in some far-coming day;
They know not what they say.

Child, gone into the sky,
To me thou 'lt never die,
The mother-life will never cease to bleed,
The mother-heart can never cease to need
Its missing morning meed.

Stay, flood of dark regret!
Sad soul, behold her yet,—
Behold her, sheltered from life's wild alarms,
Behold her, folded from thick-coming harms,
In the All-Loving Arms.

THE LITTLE BOOT.

HOW dumpy, stubbed, and old —
 The funniest little boot,
With mended toe and flattened heel,
 Ever worn by a little foot.
Within the children's room
 The widowed mother stands,
Soft-smiling down, with misty eyes,
 On a little boot in her hands.

All carefully laid away,
 With a mother's yearning care,
Are toys with which the children played,
 And the clothes they used to wear.
With loving, longing heart
 Her gaze is backward cast,
As she softly lifts the little boot
 From the stillness of the past.

She sees a little boy
   Thrust out his chubby foot,
And hears his happy shout
   At sight of his first boot;
And trudging down the road,
   Crushing grass and leaves and roots,
She sees the solid form
   Of the little man in boots.
A conquerer that day,
   He made the soft airs ring;
Mid shoeless lads at school
   The boy in boots was king.

  .   .   .   .   .

Oh, the stillness of the room
   Where the children used to play;
Oh the silence of the house,
   Since the children went away!
And this the mother-life:
   "To bear, to love, to lose,"
Till all the sweet sad tale is told
   In a pair of little shoes, —
In a single broken toy,
   In a flower pressed to keep,
All fragrant still, the faded life
   Of one who fell asleep.

The boy who wore the boot —
  While his mother's eyes are dim,
In the world's unequal strife,
  How fareth it with him?
Are the feet of manhood strong
  For manhood's sacred race, —
His hand outstretched, securely calm,
  To clasp its utmost grace?

With love her heart o'erflows,
  With love her eyes are dim,
As she silently wraps the little boot,
  And sends it far to him.

Beside his twilight fire,
  The eyes of manhood scan
The ancient boot; the far-off boy
  Talks through it with the man.
The hard world's vexing road,
  The boy's foot never pressed;
The boy knew not of manhood's pain,
  Nor felt its need of rest.

The man sees all things changed,
   The earth, the heaven above,
One thing alone remains the same
   To him — his mother's love.
The battered little boot
   He takes as from her hand,
And seems all sweetest, purest things,
   Better to understand.
This is the mother-life —
   To lose with anguish wild,
And yet live on, in every pulse,
   Forever in her child.

How dumpy, stubbèd, and old, —
   The funniest little boot,
With mended toe and flattened heel,
   Ever worn by a little foot;
Yet the boot is a bond to bind
   The man to his innocent past,
And to hold his faithful heart
   To life's first love, and its last.

NOT DEAD.*

THOU art not dead, yet when I go to seek thee,
　　And find thee not where thou wert wont to
　　　　be,
And, listening, hear the cadenced melody
　Of thy low voice — so marvellous to me —
　　　No more, no more!

Shall I too call thee dead?　Oh, shall I cry
　Through the void silence, as I moan for thee:
"Tell me, my Beautiful, why didst thou die?
　Why rise to regions where we cannot see
　　　Who love thee, — why?"

* Almina Cary Swift, the youngest sister of Alice and Phœbe
Cary.

When next I stand in the familiar room,
   And, half-expectant, by the vacant chair, —
Lay back the curtains in their purple gloom,
   To touch the golden shadow of thy hair,
     Thou wilt be there.

Yet blind me not with thy seraphic face,
   Nor seeking fingers thrill with spirit touch;
For I am mortal, and thine angel grace,
   In its beatitude, would be too much
     To see, and live.

Show me thy woman face, — the sweet, sweet face
   That I must love forever, — strong to bless,
Drawing all souls toward thee with the grace
   Of its unfathomable tenderness —
     Those eyes, those eyes!

The earth is fair, — oh lovelier, fairer far
   To all-divining sight like thine, unsealed
To spiritual meanings. Yonder star,
   Yon blade of grass, its mystery had revealed
     To thee, to thee.

Thy soul was one with Nature's.   Every vein,
  That fed the pulses of her mighty heart,
Flowed back to thine with thrill of bliss or pain;
  Her changing moods made smiles or tears
        to start
      In thy dark eyes.

Now, when the days fade, when the mornings dawn,
  And when the Springs their tender robes shall
    make,
The murmurous waves moan of a dear voice gone,
  A sweeter meaning, for thy gentle sake,
      The world will take.

Ah, now I mind me of a vanished June,
  When we, above the sad, sonorous sea,
Sat side by side, and thy deep gaze drank in
  A deeper life; from its infinity,
      It spake with thee.

You murmured, gazing on the crowning woods:
  "In such an air, and under such a sky,
Lulled by the rhythm of eternal floods,
  'T would be so holy and so sweet to die, —
      To die, and live."

I saw the luminous lifting of thine eyes,
   And trembled, — lest upon the scented sward,
Waiting to bear away my precious prize,
   Stood the invisible angel of the Lord,
     All veiled to me.

Now as I wander from my native North,
   Thou to full liberty of life hath passed;
The Emancipating Hand hath led thee forth,
   Enfranchised spirit, thou art free at last,
     No longer bound!

VANISHED FACES.

THE vanished, vanished faces
   Press on our inner sight;
We see them in the morning,
   We see them in the night.
Belovèd are the living,
   Who have not taken flight,
But the vanished, vanished faces
   Make the lonely heart's delight.

Oh the vanished, vanished faces, —
   The Baby's fairy face,
The Mother's, sweetly human,
   The Maiden's airy grace;
Oh the endless, endless patience,
   Oh the peace upon the face
Of the dear old, weary Father,
   As he neared the heavenly place!

Oh the vanished, vanished faces, —
  The ones that life hath ta'en
And set in passless distance,
  Beyond our love or pain:
We see them in our sorrow,
  We see them in our pride,
But they 're farther from us
  Than the loved ones who have died.

Life, life 's the hopeless robber,
  When it sets its iron wall
'Twixt eyes that seek each other,
  'Twixt hearts that love and call.
Oh the vanished, vanished faces
  Fill the swift-receding years,
Leaning in upon our visions,
  Touching all our smiles and tears.

FOREVER LIVES THE KING.*

A S comes back Summer mid these Winter days,
    Breathing upon us with her late sweet breath,
So com'st thou back from the mysterious ways,
    Close on the borders of the realm of death.
We looked not for her, we had said " Farewell!"
    Yet lo, she lives! and we rejoicing sing.
We cried: " The King is dead,— farewell, fare-
        well! "
    But lo, he lives to-day, still crownèd King.

Dearer this second Summer than the first;
    Dearer the pallid buds the pale suns bring,
Out of due season born, by cold skies nursed,
    Than sumptuous flowers in splendor blossoming;
Than all the blatant heroes of the year,
    Than all the noisy wrestlers of the ring, —
With visor off, with broken lance and spear,
    Thou 'rt dearer than them all, O prostrate King!

* Written to Samuel Bowles one week before his death.

No, not Farewell: forever lives the King!
  If, like this second Summer, thou pass on,
Truth, thou hast scattered, on ascending wing
  Will soar to heights thy earth-name never won, —
Reign on a throne thy kingdom gave thee not;
  Yet while with humblest man it deigns to dwell,
With care for sorrows of the common lot,
  Thou livest the King, and there is no Farewell.

The weary Winter of man's dearth and fear
  Will break at last into the bloom of Spring;
Again, again will Truth bud like the year;
  Then we will cry: "Immortal lives the King!
We see him still: he moves from star to star,
  Yet lives and reigns where transient mortals
    dwell;
Fast follow we unto the spheres afar,
  Where parting is not, there is no Farewell."

IN MEMORY:

WITH LILY AND VIOLETS.

A FAR the Northern snow is piled
    Upon his grave, to us so dear;
And yet they blossom in his name,
    These tender violets of the year.

Six years agone, this gray March morn,
    The life we love was yielded up;
The soul, so dear, to God was borne,
    Pure as this lily's stainless cup.

For us the weary days go on;
    He knows the peace for which we sigh;
His only grief that we must grieve, —
    'T is he who lives and we who die.

Only a little further on
    He 'll take thy hand, and, lifting thee
From shadow of thy mortal days,
    His face immortal thou shalt see.

Together on the heavenly heights,
    With no dark widowhood between,
Then these void days and lonely nights
    Will be as if they had not been.

The snow lies chill upon his grave,
    Yet in this Southern land these flowers
Speak sweet for him, and seem to say:
    " I wait, Love, through the painless hours,
Thy coming to the perfect day, —
    Thy coming to the perfect joy,
Wherein all tears are wiped away;
    Where, through the fair eternal years,
My Love is dying none will say."

ONE BOND.

TIME changes all; and, soon or late,
  They, who seemed one of heart,
Yield unto mightier law of fate,
  And happier walk apart.

Yet sometimes into Memory's land
  With silent steps they go,
And healing waters from her hand
  Their spirits overflow.

Beside a single grave they stand;
  The morning glow has fled, —
Yet sundered heart and parted hand
  Clasp o'er the sacred dead.

THE GUEST.

FROM out the great world's rush and din
    There came a guest:
The inner court he entered in,
    And sat at rest.

Slow on the wild tide of affairs
    The gates were closed:
Afar the hungry host of cares
    In peace reposed.

Then through the dim doors of the past,
    All pure of blame,
Came boyish memories floating fast. —
    His mother's name.

" Ah, all this loud world calls the best
          I 'd give," he said,
" To feel her hand, — on her dear breast
          To lean my head.

" I cry within the crownèd day :
          ' That would be joy,
Could she but bear me far away,
          Once more her boy.' "

Man's strength is weakness after all ;
          He stood confessed.
None quite can quell the heart's wild call,
          None all are blest.

Across the face that knows no fear
          A shade swept fast,
As if a lingering angel near
          That moment passed.

The sacred silence of the room
          Did softly stir ;
A splendor grew within the gloom —
          Of her, of *her !*

Out to the vast world's rush and din
    Hath gone my guest:
The battle, blame, the praise men win,
    Are his, — not rest.

Far out amid the world's turmoils
    A strong man stands,
Upheld in triumph, in his toils,
    By unseen hands.

But who may lift with subtle wand
    The mask we wear?
I only know his mother's hand
    Is on his hair.

I only know, through all life's harms,
    Through sin's alloy,
Somehow, *somewhere*, the mother's arms
    Will reach her boy.

ON THE FERRY.

ON the ferry, sailing over
　　To the city lying dim,
In the mellow mist of evening,
　　By the river's farthest rim;
On the ferry, gazing outward
　　To the ocean far and cold,
While the blue bay dips its waters
　　In the sunset's fleeting gold;

On the ferry, gazing outward, —
　　Motionless the great ships stand,
And above, each eager pennon
　　Lures me with a beckoning hand.
Leaning on the uneasy water,
　　Flash the sunset bars of flame,
Like the legendary ladder
　　On which angels went and came.

. . . .

In another Summer evening,
   On a little way before,
I shall reach another ferry,
   Seeking swift a farther shore;
I shall cross a drearier ferry,
   Crossing to return no more, —
Sailing for a fairer city,
   Lying on a fairer shore.

Will God's sunshine lean around me,
   Fusing every wave in gold?
Wilt thou row me gently over,
   Charon, boatman calm and cold?
When the earth-airs cease to chill me,
   When my meagre day is done,
Boatman, bear me through the splendor
   Falling from the setting sun!
Bear me outward to the mystery
   The Eternal will unfold, —
To the unrevealèd glory
   Hid within yon gates of gold.

Life may touch the soul so gently,
   We can hardly call it rough;
Yet we 'll all say, in its closing,
   Our brief day 's been long enough.
When I stand with gathered garments,
   Ere the deeper shadows fall;
When my heart drops its last idol,
   Listening for the boatman's call, —
Come! and by my spirit's sinking,
   By my shrinking fears untold,
Bear me gently o'er those waters,
   Charon, boatman calm and cold.

THE SUNSET.

ABOVE the roofs of the city,
 Above its toil and din,
The rose-red flame of the sunset
 To my chamber floweth in.
Below is the strife and tumult,
 Below is the grief and sin;
Above, the glory of sunset
 To my soul is flowing in.

I tire, I tire of the warfare;
 I tire of striving to win;
The soul of my life's high purpose
 Calls no high hope its kin.
Ambition's bay-crowned ladder,
 That leans against the sky, —
I am too tired to climb it,
 It towers so steep and high;
And I cannot see above me,
 So dense the shadows lie.

THE SUNSET.

Lonely I droop in the darkness,
  Weary I pray for rest;
Lo, light of a sudden glory
  Breaks on my clouded breast!
Like the kindling of the sunset
  Above earth's gloom and sin,
Every shadow gloweth golden
  As the splendor floweth in.
The light of God's own promise
  Shines on my purpose high;
I rise and wrestle upward,
  With a faith that cannot die.

SLEEP.

BELOVED Sleep, drop low thy veil,—
    I would not hear, I would not see;
Let all the daytime pictures pale,
    And all its voices die to me.

From wounding words, the scourging rods
    That smite the heart in paltry day,
O Somnus, gentlest of the gods,
    Bear thou me far, oh far away!

Bear thou me on, beyond my fates,
    To yon dim palace of thy reign;
For where the soul of Silence waits,
    I may forget my mortal pain.

I'll lie beneath thy dusky plumes,
 And Night from poppied hand will cast,
Far down the void Lethean glooms,
 The sunless sorrows of my past.

And in thy drowsy air will cease
 The soul's deep cry, the voiceless sigh;
While youth's sweet dreams, new-born of peace,
 Round all my royal couch shall lie.

REST.

WEEP not when I am dead, dear friend;
   Sweetheart, grieve not when I lie low;
While o'er my clay your soft eyes bend,
   Remember it was good to go.
When low you press the violet sod,
   Whose purple tears enstar my breast,
Belovèd, think I sleep in God,
   Remember such alone are blest.

The perfect silence will be dear,
   How dear the chance of painless rest;
And on, beyond all pain or fear,
   The perfect waking will be best.
How dim this distant day will seem,
   How far the grief we suffer here!
This life the mirage of a dream,
   Merged to a morning calm and clear.

WASTE?

HOW much must go for naught! How many
    tears,
  All wept in silence, are yet wept in vain;
Unmoved go on the swift, relentless years;
  The one we pray for never knows our pain.

How much must go for naught! E'en beauteous
    youth
  Turns from its kingdom, laying down its crown,
Crying for what it yields. It went in sooth,
  The promised fruitage, with the flower's first
    down.

How much must go for naught! The Summer
    years,
  So rich in struggle, rich in hoarded faith;
Even Fulfilment, Failure stings and sears;
  Slain Expectation dies reluctant death.

Yet somewhere, *somewhere*, O most tender Lord,
  Sure Thou dost count them for us, treasure all;
Life's futile toil, joy missed, the sweet, lost word,
  The love that loves in vain, the tears that fall.

DISCORD.

SWIFT through the fragrant air it fell,
  A single word;
The wound it made no word may tell, —
  For no one heard
Save one sweet heart, whose very life
  Is love and truth.
This heart the word pierced like a knife;
  No pulse of ruth
Thrilled him who aimed the cruel word;
  He willed and spoke;
A fair face quivered, soft lips stirred,
  A fond heart broke.

Alas! the springtime air is full
  Of wrathful words;
They rise to heaven, and would annul
  The sweet-voiced birds,

That everywhere on glancing wing
　　Fly from the south,
New messages of love to bring
　　With open mouth.

Nature's glad face the sons of men
　　Doth put to shame.
She says : " Poor children of the earth,
　　Why strive and blame?
You work and war, — the will of fate
　　Abides the same !
The purposes of God survive
　　Your feeble fray ;
You cannot change them though you shrive
　　Your sins alway.
The name you toil for may outlive
　　Your little day,
But you must live when earth and name
　　Have fled away.
Drink thou my sunshine, breathe my air,
　　Ere yet too late ;
Take thou, with soul serene and fair,
　　Thine high estate ! "

The placid seasons o'er earth's breast
　　　Move to and fro;
Unscared its birds brood in their nest;
　　　Its wood-flowers blow
In peace above its stormiest crest.
　　　In God's good plan,
His loveliest creatures all find rest
　　　Take thine, O man!

REPROOF.

No word sails soft upon the air
  Sweet with approval.   Far aloof
'T would hold me from the grief I bear;
  Thy silence is thy keen reproof.

I hear no wounding word of blame,
  No mandate with its high behoof,
No taunt, with withering fang of flame, —
  Silence, alas! is thy reproof.

Afar the face of symbolled saint
  Bends low beneath the mystic roof;
I feel, through prayer and praise and plaint,
  The silence stern of thy reproof.

Thy grave, grand words, the holy past
  Doth hold as jewels in its woof;
Thy consecrated speech must last
  Beyond thy silence, thy reproof.

SILENCE

DOWN through the starry intervals,
    Upon this weary-laden world,
How soft the soul of Silence falls!
How deep the spell wherewith she thralls;
    How wide her mantle is unfurled!

She broods o'er the bewildering street:
    Lo, day's turmoil and strivings cease;
She folds in sleep its rushing feet;
On traffic, racing loud and fleet,
    She sets the signet of her peace.

The world is full of weary noise,
    The dreary discords of the air;
Their cry, the charm of life destroys,
They jar the spirit from its poise,
    These human voices harsh with care.

Within the city's prisoning room
    My spirit roams by hill and flood;
Feels twilight's hush, its tender gloom,
The silence of the grasses' bloom,
    The peace of nature deep and good!

Dear Silence, weary soul and brain —
    In every age with thee apart —
Have prayed thee heal the pulse of pain,
When friends drop off, when love lies slain, —
    The low, slow aching of the heart.

Of all our loving Father's gifts,
    I often wonder which is best,
And cry: " Dear God, the one that lifts
    Our soul from weariness to rest,
    The rest of Silence, — that is best."

I deem a little farther on —
    Though morn or eve I cannot tell —
We 'll halt, our long day's journey done,
    And softly murmur: " It is well, —
God's perfect Silence, — it is won."

LOSS.

ONLY so much the less, —
   One heart has fallen away;
It took no light from the sun,
   No splendor out of the day.
The sunshine seems the same,
   And the opal tints on the sea,
And the golden-rod's yellow flame,
   Yet something has gone from me.

One heart, one heart the less
   When I name the names of my friends;
One love, that seemed born to bless,
   In a mirage of falsehood ends.
The sunshine seems the same,
   And the opal tints on the sea,
And the golden-rod's yellow flame, —
   Yet something has gone from me.

KNOWLEDGE.

IN what rare region of the mind
  Shall I yet know thee as thou art, —
The holier self I fain would find,
  Above the market and the mart?

My yearning life goes forth to meet
  Thy loftier spirit, all unseen, —
Afar, illusive, mocking, sweet,
  With all the body's veil between.

Then, in all lowliness, I 'd show
  The gentler life I live apart;
But dim thou only seest it glow,
  Through some infirmity of heart.

Yet, in how many a gift and grace,
　　The inner sight doth catch the gleam
Cast from the hidden angel's face, —
　　The lovelier self of whom we dream.

The nearest stand and knock without,
　　The dearest walk so far apart;
Comes withering fear and cruel doubt
　　'Twixt life and life, 'twixt heart and heart.

All mortal shadow swept away, —
　　The clouded night, the questioning eye, —
I deem, in some supernal day,
　　The best in each will each descry.

Lo! lifted from the earth's turmoil,
　　From every curse of care or fate,
In yon rare region of the soul
　　Our hearts redeemed must meet and mate.

THE YACHTS.

WE stood upon the ocean cliffs,
   And softly wondered who would win,
As, out beyond the waiting skiffs,
   We watched two stately yachts sail in.

Abreast they spread their eager sail—
   The gentle southern breezes blew —
Till, caught by one victorious gale,
   Far on the lovely Phantom flew.

All gorgeously the evening sun
   Slid swiftly downward to the bay,
And through the twilight's gathering gold
   We saw the Cambria far away.

All homeward came the racing skiffs,
   No longer wondering who would win,
As underneath the purple cliffs
   We saw the Phantom gliding in.

I stand upon the downs of life,
   And watch two barks of Fate sail in;
The waves and winds are all at strife,
   I sadly wonder who will win, —

Who, caught by Fortune's favoring gales,
   Will sail in sooner, proud and fast,
And who, with conquered, silent sails,
   Must gain the blessèd harbor last.

BY THE SEA.

UPON the lonely shore I lie;
   The wind is faint, the tide is low,
Someway there seems a human sigh
   In the great waves that inward flow, —

As if all love, and loss, and pain,
   That ever swept their shining track,
Had met within the caverned main,
   And, rising, moaningly come back.

Upon the lonely shore I lie,
   And gaze along its level sands.
Still from the sea steals out the cry
   I left afar in crowded lands.

Upon the sea-beach, cool and still,
   I press my cheek; and yet I hear
The jar of earth, and catch the thrill
   Of human effort, hot and near.

Come, Peace of nature! Lone I lie
   Within the calm Midsummer noon.
All human want I fain would fly,
   Sing Summer sea in silvery croon!

In Noon's great gladness hush thy moan,
   In vast possession unbereft;
No music, haunting all thy tone,
   Can make me want the world I 've left.

ROOM.

ROLL back, O World, just like the tide,
    Now wavering outward from my feet;
Leave for mine eyes the margin wide,
    Where truth and love have room to meet.

Roll back, thou World! — the peering crowd,
    With eyes attent; sad Envy's lees
Filtered through speech, the laughter loud, —
    Give me the largeness of the seas.

On this vast vantage-ground I stand;
    The World rolls back, just like the tide.
I measure, with unerring hand,
    Its mite bestowed, its wealth denied.

Circled by yon horizon vast,
   How easy to be great and free!
All littleness of life I cast
   In the great hollow of the sea.

" Roll back, O World! " I still will cry,
   When close life presses, strong and sweet.
Room is there, 'twixt the sea and sky,
   For truth and nobleness to meet.

I MIGHT HAVE DONE.

IS there a sadder word than this,
   " I might have done "?
I might have filled life's cup of bliss,
   At least for one!

" I might have done!"   So simple joy —
   Love's word or wile —
Robs life of half its sad alloy,
   Makes life a smile.

" I might have done!"   While young life
      strewed
   Her prescient seeds,
Each folded germ, with life endued,
   To bloom in deeds.

O love-fraught Hours, sail mutely on;
    Die, one by one;
'T is life to sigh, when all are gone:
    " I might have done!"

TWO ANGELS.

TWO angels met above my pillow.
   One bore within her arms
The fears and griefs which haunt my spirit.
   And all the dead day's harms.

The other, bending low above her,
   Though seeming farther down,
Held all the joys and tendernesses
   My weary day had known.

I said: "O angel of my sorrows,
   I 'm weary of regret!
Why haunt me still with pangs and losses
   My heart would fain forget?"

Then softly said the other angel:
    "Look higher unto me,
And all this human pain and passion
    Thine eyes will cease to see.

"Look unto me, Time's grieving daughter;
    See, in the midnight air,
A vision that will swiftly show thee
    That still thy life is fair."

Slow-shaping in the purple dimness
    I saw a distant face;
And the deep eyes were full of sadness
    And Love's beseeching grace.

Then gently said my better angel:
    "Why dost thy heart repine?
Why dost thou sit in doubt and shadow,
    While faith and love are thine?

"For thou hast strength for all thy crosses,
    Joy for thy saddest part,
If thou canst live, through pain and losses,
    Safe in one faithful heart.

7

" For they alone have need of sorrow,
   And they alone are poor,
For whom, in life, Love's holy angel
   Hath opened not her door."

How near from out the midnight dimness
   Shone the belovèd face ;
And the deep eyes were full of gladness —
   Love's beatific grace.

Where now the dark and distant anguish
   Left by a desolate day?
I looked.   Lo ! the discordant angel
   Had fled in shame away.

ONE DEATH.

VOID of Faith's ennobling crown,
    Lies a dead Love in my breast.
In its grave I laid it down;
    It is dead, so let it rest.
Once it gave life richer zest,
    More than any joy beside;
Yet I buried it — 't was best;
    Shall I tell you why it died?

Would 't were — better to pretend —
    Dead; 't is sacred as it seemed;
But 't is thus — the idol friend
    Was less noble than I deemed.
Love whose love all self transcends,
    Love, in loving strong as death,
Cannot bide a treacherous friend,
    Dies beside its murdered faith.

Thus we wake some saddened morn,
　　And, in silence, put aside
One for whom we once seemed born,
　　One for whom we could have died.
In some morning further on,
　　We shall meet, and I will say:
"Thou, my being leaned upon,
　　Nothing art to me to-day."

Loved one, lying in the dust,
　　I bewept you with no pain:
For we parted, with the trust,
　　In God's morn to meet again.
· But a deeper woe is born
　　When we know our faith has fled:
Dawns no resurrection morn
　　On the love which lieth dead.

God's dear world is just as fair —
　　Sky and sea and circling coast;
Glory of the earth and air,
　　Do you miss what I have lost?

No rare form I lay away,
   Cherished more than all beside;
'T is a love — it died to-day;
   I have told you why it died.

VALERY.

VALERY gazed toward the setting sun;
 Fair was Valery, fair to see.
She laid her brown hands one on one,
 And sat as still as a girl could be.

Far gazed Valery; no one came.
 Lonely the great red sun dropped down,
And the mountain caught its oriflamme,
 And flashed its radiance, crown on crown.

Soft sighed Valery: " Far thou art
 Over the mountain; and far away
Dwelleth the knight who stole my heart.
 ' He will never come back,' the people say.

"Then woe is me," sad Valery said;
    "How can I live without my heart?
He carried it with him. I'd better be dead,
    Than to live from my life and my love apart.

"O Summer twilight, O fragrant wood, —
    Far back in the silence, dear and dim,
Where in sweeter words than I understood,
    He said I was all the world to him!

"The world!" sighed Valery. "I am afraid
    Of yon grand world where my hero dwells.
'T is full of jeweled and beautiful maids,
    And riches and honors, the story tells."

What, in the splendor of all his days,
    Can Valery be? Such a lowly one —
With her work-brown hands and homely ways —
    Will soar and sink like a mote in his sun.

"Ah, woe is me!" sweet Valery said, —
    And fair was Valery, fair to see, —
"I would that I had been safely dead
    Before my heart had gone out from me —

"To an alien world with an idle knight,
  Gone and left me to moan and moan.
I'd go and lie down in the river to-night,
  But I fear to sin and to die alone."

            .   .   .   .

The mountain glows to an amethyst;
  The tree boughs vein the sky's deep gold.
Under the maples, unto his tryst,
  Cometh a rider swift and bold!

"Sweet, my Valery, waiting alone!
  Fair, my Valery, fair to see!
One, *one* Valery in the world,
  And she is all of the world to me!

"*Afraid?* Afraid that the great world might
  Lure me away, sweetheart, from you?
That jeweled maidens, in splendor dight,
  Could be more than one woman pure and true?

"Perchance to many! never to him
  Who loveth one for herself alone;
Your hair may fade and your eyes grow dim,
  And you will be, Valery, *more* my own."

Still in the rays of the setting sun
 Sitteth our Valery, fair to see;
Her brown hands, folded one on one,
 Are lying in peace on her husband's knee.

THE GOOD ANGEL.

O GOOD angel in the air,
    Lovely soul, redeemed and holy, —
Come you from your mansions fair
    To this earth-home, poor and lowly?

Yester-eve one softly said:
    " Rare the dower you inherit;
Evermore above your head
    Floats a pure celestial spirit.

" Hidden from the common sight,
    Hidden from the world's derision, —
Help for you, by day or night,
    Shines she on my inner vision."

Now the sunset spills its red,
   Now the twilight gold is paling,
In the silence o'er my head
   Is the silent angel sailing.

In the dimness on me shed,
   In the darkness round me falling,
In your human voice's stead,
   Do I hear your soul-voice calling?

I have never seen your face
   Since it wore its earth-light tender;
Veiled for me your angel-grace,
   And your eyes' seraphic splendor.

I no more can cry for pain
   That your life-bark from me drifted;
I shall never sigh again
   That your veil of life was lifted.

Not alone that you have gone
   From the tempting and the sinning;
Not alone that you have won,
   Past all wanting and all winning!

Weak and wavering, the will
 Falters in the dark come o'er me;
O dear angel, near me still,
 Show the true way on before me!

All of evil, all of ill,
 From the gold of good you 've sifted,
With your light anoint me till
 I, too, see the veil uplifted.

Human fear will cease to prey
 On a soul so held and tended;
Souls of evil drop away
 From a spirit so defended.

All the human, fainting still,
 You can kindle and inspire;
All the faltering spirit fill
 With your fine seraphic fire.

Seek I ne'er to see your face,
 Nor your eyes' supernal splendor;
All enough that God's dear grace
 Made a seraph, me to lend her.

'T is enough that all the air
   Trembles with your still evangel,
That my narrow house of care
   Yet hath room to hold an angel.

MY PLACE.

STILL keep my place for me, dear friends,
  While absent days wane wearily;
Though lovelier eyes their love-light lend,
  Still keep my place for me!

I keep your places, every one,
  When gala-days with beauty bless;
When lonely days move slowly on,
  I love you more, not less.

The precious presence, needed much,
  Low love-words set to silvery speech,
Love's glance of eye, love's thrill of touch,
  Have passed to memories each.

And now I mind me how 't is said
　　That hearts that love apart grow cold;
And yet I find no newer love
　　That 's dearer than the old.

Though still I take from every hour
　　The task it giveth me to do,
And love and nurse joy's tiniest flower,
　　That blossoms in its dew;

Something of beauty from the day,
　　Something of perfume from the flower,
I seem to miss, — and sigh and say,
　　" I miss my love's lost dower! "

I mourn the eyes I cannot see,
　　I mourn the tones that used to bless;
For only rich this life can be
　　In love and tenderness.

I rob no other heart; I flee
　　All love save mine by claim divine, —
The lavish love poured out for me
　　Only because 't is mine!

My life-threads, myriad-tinted, see!
　　I seek to weave, with patient hand,
To beauteous woof of harmony,
　　The many-shaded strand.

Sometimes, amid the silent dearth,
　　I'm tired: I say, " The task is long."
Oh, do you miss me in your mirth,
　　And miss me in your song?

And need me, as in dear gone days?
　　Whose lovelier eyes, whose fairer face,
Whose hands fulfil my ministries?
　　Who fills my vacant place?

The sunset's limpid amber blends
　　With flowing azure of the sea;
Far gazing out, I cry: " Sweet friends,
　　Still keep my place for me! "

And gazing upward to the sky,
　　Where all God's golden glories be,
The many-mansioned house on high
　　I strain my eyes to see.

" I will prepare a place for thee ! "
   Dear promise of the tender Word !
Their place Thine exiled children see
   With Thee, belovèd Lord !

Thus, when my human spirit faints,
   And tired feet droop wearily,
Still with the lowliest of Thy saints,
   Lord, keep a place for me !

8

IDLE.

THE flush of Autumn on the woods,
    The Autumn splendor in the sky,
The strong rush of its risen floods, —
    Idle I see these days go by.

I shut my eyes. How close I see
    My long-time haunts: the cedar grove,
The hollows where the fine ferns be,
    The maiden-hair, — the leaves I love.

Ye wait in vain in hush or hum,
    O fairy ferns, O leaves of gold,
O piney paths so sweet and dumb!
    Your lover comes not as of old.

IDLE.

But here beside the dissonant sea,
   I list its chant, its plaint of pain,
And ask if ways so dear to me
   Will ever know my feet again.

Thou crying sea, thou hungry main, —
   How like this world's unresting mass!
Vaulting desire that 's never slain,
   And moaning want that cannot pass.

Give me the silence of the hills,
   Their calm uplifting deep and vast,
The timbre of the mountain-rills,
   Glories of Autumns that are past.

    .   .   .   .   .

The Winter pallor on the world,
   The Winter splendor in its sky,
White banners of the frost unfurled, —
   Idle I see these days go by.

I hear the thunder of the mart,
   See scheming sparrows scold and fly;
I trace, within the heaven's rich heart,
   The primrose dawn, the twilight dye.

Beyond them all, yet close and clear,
     Come echoes of the world's gay feet;
The murmur of my world I hear,
     I see its phantoms far and fleet.

I feel the rush of grand affairs, —
     The eager quest, the careless crowd,
The heavy cross of secret cares,
     The daytime dance, the laughter loud.

I watch this far-off world go by;
     It needeth not *one* tender heart,
One busy hand, one worker's sigh, —
     I know it as I sit apart.

I chafe not at its fickle shows;
     Dear is this silence, full of peace,
This foretaste of the long day's close,
     When work and hate and love shall cease.

                .   .   .   .

Spring's firstling flowers in spicèd hoods,
     Spring's iridescence in the sky,
The life-throb of her muffled buds, —
     Idle I see these days go by.

Yet dear the calm that round me thrills,
    The ether of this upper sky;
For she who waits, as she who wills,
    Is dear to God, I know not why.

LAST ROSES.

I PLUCK from pale November air
   The last, sad roses of the year;
Roses of June were not more fair,
   Whose bloom of joy evoked no tear.

Alas! in chillness, in the frost,
   Ye darlings, woke your pallid bloom;
Yet not a hint of fragrance lost
   Floats through the stillness of my room.

The last, the last! To-morrow's snow
   Will fall upon your Summer bed,
And homeless winds despairing flow
   Where rose the radiance of each head.

Close-folded in your emerald hoods,
 What loving quest, what tender gloom,
Is yours, ye mute, appealing buds,
 In beauty born, but not to bloom.

Triumphal blossoms of the June,
 I see your iridescence stain
The limpid azure, hear the tune
 A bird then sang, — hope's gay refrain.

O sweet was Summer, — sweet the word
 The roses in the garden spoke !
The prophecies, the faith, they stirred
 In thee, O heart, as high noon broke.

Yet here is Autumn lone and late;
 And here its roses, fair as Spring,
And sweet as if no alien fate
 Had touched with frost their blossoming.

Their lovely petals fall apart,
 All trembling at my word of praise;
In fragrance deep each sweet, void heart
 Its cup of blessing mute doth raise.

Like June, yet different, — here is all;
   No hope waits hidden in these buds.
No promise, as these petals fall,
   The space with all its splendor floods.

Heart, — thicker than these fallen leaves
   Cluster thy hopes, born all too late;
What sunless morns, what long, cold eves,
   What frost hath sealed their piteous fate!

Accept thine Autumn, bare and gray,
   Its wounded life, its tender gloom, —
Its roses reft of June's warm ray,
   Its folded buds that cannot bloom.

Dearer than heraldry of Spring,
   Than fruitage glad of all the years,
The love that cannot lift its wing,
   The faded flower wet with tears.

The blossom, of earth's promise shorn,
   Still sends its incense to the sky;
And Love, of heavenly patience born,
   To Love of Love at last must fly.

THE HERMIT-THRUSH.

O HERMIT-THRUSH, one August day,
 I heard from out thy golden throat
('T was long ago and far away)
 Thy song supernal fall and float.

A weary pilgrim by the road,
 I deemed some passing seraph's strain
Was falling on my heavy load —
 In heavenly music sweet to pain.

'T was long ago and far away;
 The life I lived that hour has fled;
The pang that pierced, that Summer day,
 Has ceased to hurt, forever dead.

Yet lo! once more by leafy way
  I hear thy lone, seraphic strain;
The pomp of all the Summer day
  Thrills with thy music sweet to pain.

What if youth's Spring be early gone, —
  If joy be tardy, dawning late, —
Thou singest of Summer joys unknown,
  Of higher heights.   Lo, calm I wait!

O bird, from off Heaven's inmost shrine
  Adown to earth thou bearest to me
One note from out the strain divine,
  Prophet of love, of life to be!

Yet further on, some later even,
  I 'll catch once more thy mateless strain,
Thou lovely messenger from Heaven,
  Bearing its music sweet to pain.

'T will reach me on my lowly road,
  Thy call, Heaven's last, so far, so fine,
Lifting my heart from mortal load,
  From love in loss, to love divine.

THE DOVES.

UNDERNEATH the homestead window
    Flock the doves!
Tremulous-crested, opal-breasted,
    Household doves;
Just as when a little maiden
  Fed and called them once her loves.

Underneath the homestead window
    Low they grieve;
Looking, nodding, with a timid
    Make-believe
Of a welcome to the wanderer,
  Calling in the purple eve.

.   .   .   .   .

Like the doves unto my window
    Flocking home,
All the memories of my lifetime
    Thronging come,
Once more brooding in my bosom,
    Here in the old houschold home.

Far against the dim horizon
    See they soar, —
Hills of home, far mountains crowning,
    .   Far-off shore!
Distant as my native hilltops
    Seems the child-life gone before.

'T is the old, oft-murmured story, —
    Lost or dead!
Doubly dead are many living,
    Further fled;
I, at high noon, stand a stranger,
    With the homestead overhead.

Flock the doves beneath my window
    Just the same,
Tremulous-crested, opal-breasted,
    Shy and tame;
Who is she who calls and feeds them,
    With far sight and soul of flame?

   .   .   .   .   .

Back unto the city's rattle
    Slow I go;
'T is the bivouac, not the battle,
    I would know;
Peace of God and peace of Nature
    Feed me in their overflow.

Underneath my Southern windows
    Rolls the world,
Glancing eyelids, flowing tresses,
    Ribbons furled;
Flashing onward through the sunshine.
    Dreamed-of, ever-longed-for world!

Through the city's shifting splendor
    I shall see,
Near and clear, this twilight picture,
    Dear to me;
I shall stand in all the tumult
    Solitary, still, and free.

I shall know unto this window
    Still you come;
I shall see you, household dovelings,
    Flocking home!
I will leave the loud world for you,
    How so far my feet may roam.

Flock the doves unto Thy window,
    Lord of love!
Call us, feed us, fold us safely,
    Lest we rove.
Crowding home, Thy wandering children,
    Hungry, seek the hand above.

FALL IN.*

SEE, see, yon gleaming line of light!
    The enemy's bayonets bristle bright;
O boys, there 'll be a fight to-night;
        Fall in!

Under these woods of frozen larch,
Under the night sky's icy arch,
It ends at last, the dreadful march;
        Fall in!

Fall in!   No bivouac to-night.
Beneath the stars so still and bright,
The glistening bayonets glitter white;
        Fall in!

* Written within sight of the two American armies, in the
midst of battle, 1863.

Fall in! we're hungry, bruised, and torn, —
With snow and rain, beaten and worn, —
Yet " ready for duty," we've proudly sworn;
   Fall in!

A second for dreams!   Under our eyes,
Oh see, how softly they seem to rise,
The hills of home, and her Summer skies!
   · Fall in!

One sigh for home, — for the fair face prest
Close to the heart, 'neath the rugged vest,
The face of the one we love the best;
   Fall in!

O say, — for a flash shall the brown face pale,
The quick young nerves in their warm life
  quail,
To meet the thud of the leaden hail?
   Fall in!

The storm of shells, the bullet's whir,
The clash of sabre, — no fear can stir;
We fight for freedom, for home, for *her;*
   Fall in!

Ever with steady step we go,
With rifles ready in serried row,
Into the face of the insolent foe;
    Fall in!

Our hearts upleap in passionate pain, —
Oh see, they fall, our heroic slain;
The enemy's masses charge and gain!
    Fall in!

Fall in! the eager bugles beat;
Fall in! march on with prescient feet;
Smite low the foe where the armies meet;
    Fall in!

To front! its ranks are red and thin,
The victor flaunts his banner of sin;
O comrades, forward! to die, or win;
    Fall in!

A BALLAD OF THE BORDER.

TELL you a story, Johnny, my knight?
  A story of what? Of the march, or the
    fight?

I 'll fasten the shutter, and pile the brands higher,
And banish the storm in the flame of the fire.

Johnny, my darling, you 're sheltered and warm;
Hear in the valley the voice of the storm?

One year ago the winds and the damps
Crept through the crannies of circling camps,

And the frozen ground was the only bed
Where the war-worn soldier could lay his head.

And all night long, on the breastwork's " beat,"
We heard the sound of the sentinel's feet.

Beside the Potomac's echoing flood,
Through pitiless storms our pickets stood.

Grim guns from the mountain-tops looked down,
Solemnly guarding the ancient town.

All our defenders their watch would keep,
That little Johnnies like you might sleep.

Now for the story!   Johnny, my king,
Shall it make tears run, or your merry laugh ring?

Here in the valley there used to be
Two young brothers, most fair to see.

They were born of a stately and lofty race, —
Grew tall, and straight, and strong in their grace.

As gay as their steeds, and as free of care,
Were Allen and Algernon Monclare.

They had grown to young manhood's power and
      state
When Virginia rushed to her traitor-fate,

And broke the bond of her ancient troth,
Because Carolina was foolish and wroth.

"I'll fight with my State," said Algernon fair;
"I'll die for my Country," said Allen Monclare.

Each turned his face, went his separate way —
One in Loyal blue, one in Rebel gray.

   .   .   .   .   .

Over the river, on Loudon's height,
The boys in blue pitched their tents one night.

The white camp gleamed on the rugged steep,
That we in the valley in peace might sleep.

For we knew the guerillas were coming down,
To fire at will on the sleeping town.

Low on the edge of the wooded hill
Stood the waiting pickets, alone and still.

By the smouldering camp-fire every one
Was lying at watch, each man on his gun.

"Fire!" Then the foe, with a sudden yell,
Broke the ambush like hounds of hell.

"Fire! They're upon us; up, my men!
Fire! What they give us give back again."

Face to the foe in the woody lair,
He fought with his men, Allen Monclare.

"I die for my Country — far better so,"
He said, and fell at the feet of his foe.

"Thus perish each Northern mother's son —
Cursèd invaders!" cried Algernon.

Alas, the dead! in the starlight dim
The fair young face looked up at him.

"O God!   My brother!   O terrible fate!
I loved you well.   Too late, too late!

" I 've murdered my brother!   What now can be
Southern freedom, or State, to me?"

With our buried braves on yonder hill
Allen Monclare lies white and still.

In a foreign land, afar from his slain,
Algernon carries the curse of Cain.

.   .   .   .   .

Johnny, my boy, you 're sheltered and warm;
Hear in the valley the voice of the storm.

To-morrow the sun, serene and bland,
Will kiss the mountain of Maryland.

The cruel scars on its brave old head
Will bloom as if they had never bled.

Thus the tempest of war down the valley passed,
But the morning brought sun and song at last.

The pangs of Virginia's wounds will cease,
And her scars all heal in the balm of peace.

No longer the clear stars hang their lamps
Over the dreamers in comfortless camps.

No longer the homesick pickets stand
Under the Heights of Maryland.

No longer the clear, sweet bugles call
At the dawning morn and the starlight's fall.

No longer we wake in the midnight still
To the tramp of troops on the stony hill.

No moaning drums, with their low, slow beat,
Sob for the lost in the sad defeat.

Many a brave young heart is still,
Under the snow, on the lonely hill.

Many a gallant boy to-night
Tells at home the tale of the fight.

So, Johnny my hero, the war is done,
And at last a holy peace is won.

High on the Heights of Maryland, see!
It waves over all, the Flag of the Free!

VIRGINIA, 1865.

THE JOURNALIST.*

M AN of the eager eyes and teeming brain, —
    Small is the honor that men dole to thee;
They snatch the fruitage of thy years of pain, —
    Devour, yet scorn, the tree.

What though the treasure of thy nervous force,
    Thy rich vitality of mind and heart,
Goes swiftly down before thy Moloch's course, —
    Men cry, " It is not Art ! "

The Poet, — dallying with his fitful Muse,
    On lagging Pegasus, whose halting stride
Sometimes gives out, — he scorns " the man of
        news," —
    Cries, " See ! we 're parted wide ! "

* Written by request, and read before the New York Press
Association, Utica, New York, June 8, 1881.

The Novelist — elate from lofty crest
   Of Fiction's lovely palace of the air —
Looks down and sighs: " Only a Journalist !
    My height is his despair."

The jays minute of feebler Literature —
   Who lightly chatter, on its outmost rim,
Of naught but of their small position sure —
    Point scornfully at *him !*

The Statesman — smirched, with pallid malice grim,
   Or red with wrath — doth in the morning read
Of fair faith bartered, of fine honor dim,
    In his recorded deed.

Lo, look for thunder then ! His fierce reply
   In House or Senate, as he leads the van ;
Time-server and place-seller — loud his cry :
    " Down, cursed Newspaper Man ! "

Who takes the daily journal, cool and damp,
   And weighs its ceaseless toll on nerve and brain ?
Nor morning sun, nor genial evening lamp,
    Reveals its birth of pain.

" Only a newspaper ! " Quick read, quick lost,
　Who sums the treasure that it carries hence?
Torn, trampled under feet, who counts thy cost,
　　Star-eyed Intelligence?

And ye, the Nameless, best-belovèd host !
　My heart recalls more than one vanished face,
Struck from the rank of toilers, — early lost,
　　And leaving not a trace.

Martyrs of News, young martyrs of the Press, —
　Princes of giving from largess of brain !
One leaf of laurel, steeped in tenderness,
　　Take ye, O early-slain.

Though in the Authors' Pantheon no niche
　　obscure
　Your waning names can hold forever fast,
The seeds of Truth ye blew afar are sure
　　To spring and live at last.

On lonely wastes, within the swarming marts,
　In silent dream, in speaking deeds of men, —
Quick with momentum from your deathless hearts,
　　Your thoughts will live again.

O living Journalist, — when faith hath fled,
 When men crush men amid the thick of strife, —
Bethink thee of one Man, divine, who said,
  " I am the Truth, the Life ! "

Leave Science, leave Philosophy its crown ;
 Yet sweeter ever must be that man's sleep
Who, still his mother's boy, prays, lying down,
  His Lord, his soul to keep.

Whate'er our prizes, or how fair our crown
 Or deep our losses, only this is best, —
The soul's great peace.   Nor sneer, nor smile, nor
   frown
  Can shake it from its rest.

Exalt thy calling !   On its spotless shield
 Write truth, write honor, valor, first and last.
Cravens may clutch thy stars, and thou not yield ;
  Love them, and hold them fast !

Thus Greeley wrought in fresh, heroic youth ;
 Thus Margaret Fuller wrote her way to power ;
Thus Bowles — unvanquished in a rain of ruth —
  Went down in manhood's flower.

Thus Curtis writes, — rare Sidney of the pen, —
 O'Reilly sings, and Godkin draws his steel;
Thus Schurz his highest honor takes again,
  To write the truth we feel.

Defender of the People, of the State,
 Kindler and quickener of majestic thought, —
Sure of thy finest triumph, thou canst wait
  The crown thy patience wrought.

To serve thy generation, this thy fate:
 "Written in water," swiftly fades thy name;
But he who loves his kind does, first and late,
  A work too great for fame.

L O V E.

L O V E.

———•◦•———

WORDS FOR PARTING.

Oh what shall I do, dear,
 In the coming years, I wonder,
When our paths, which lie so sweetly near,
 Shall lie so far asunder?
Oh what shall I do, dear,
 Through all the sad to morrows,
When the sunny smile has ceased to cheer
 That smiles away my sorrows?

What shall I do, my friend,
 When you are gone forever?
My heart its eager need will send
 Through the years, to find you never.

10

And how will it be with you,
  In the weary world, I wonder!
Will you love me with a love as true,
  When our paths lie far asunder?

A sweeter, sadder thing,
  My life, for having known you;
Forever with my sacred kin,
  My soul's soul, I must own you, —
Forever mine, my friend,
  From June to life's December, —
Not mine to have or hold,
  But to pray for and remember.

The way is short, O friend,
  That reaches out before us;
God's tender heavens above us bend,
  His love is smiling o'er us.
A little while is ours,
  For sorrow or for laughter;
I 'll lay the hand you love in yours,
  On the shore of the hereafter.

GOOD-BY, SWEETHEART.

GOOD-BY, Sweetheart!
    I leave thee with the loveliest things
The beauty-burdened springtime brings —
The anemone in snowy hood,
The sweet arbutus in the wood;
And to the smiling skies above
I say, " Bend brightly o'er my love; "
And to the perfume-breathing breeze
I sigh, " Sing softest symphonies."
O lutelike leaves of laden trees,
Bear all your sweet refrain to him,
While in the June-time twilights dim
He thinks of me, as I of him.
And so Good-by, Sweetheart.

Good-by, Sweetheart!
I leave thee with all purest things,
That when some fair temptation sings
Its luring song, though sore beset,

Thou 'lt stronger be.   Then no regret
Life-long will after follow thee.
With touches lighter than the air,
I kiss thy forehead brave and fair,
And say to God this last deep prayer:
" O guard him always, night and day,
So from Thy peace he shall not stray."
And so Good-by, Sweetheart.

Good-by, Sweetheart, we seem to part;
Yet still within my inmost heart
Thou goest with me.   Still my place
I hold in thine by love's dear grace;
Yet all my life seems going out,
As slow I turn my face about,
To go alone another way, —
To be alone till life's last day,
Unless thy smile can light my way.
Good-by, Sweetheart.   The dreaded dawn,
That tells our love's long tryst is gone,
Is purpling all the pallid sky,
As low I sigh, Sweetheart, Good-by.

PRESENCE.

ONE week ago to-night, O Love, we sat
    Together. Now wide miles do part us two.
And so I hail each passing cloud, and say:
"Where is he? Has thy whiteness sheltered him?"
And every pilgrim breeze that sinks to rest
Beside me, low I greet, and sigh: " Sweet wind,
Didst kiss his eyelids ere you came to me?"
Two confluent rivers, blending into one,
Go down the girded valley, mountain-walled.
Through affluent fringe of interbraiding trees
Their married voices say, "We go to him!"
O happy rivers, sliding down the vale,
Pause not to murmur mid your gardened isles,
Nor pause to play upon your reedy flutes,
Nor pause to sleep on mossy pillows low;
Flow, wedded rivers, swift to meet my Love,

And sing again to him the song I sing!
Sing, rapturous rivers, till his spirit thrills
To hear sweet echoes of my discontent,
To know that I need all in needing him.
Thou knowest I need all things, needing thee,
As lone by open window I gaze out
And see God's infinite spaces mock my sight,
And watch God's miracles still going on;
See soft nights die, and tranquil mornings born
In tender silence on the sacred hills;
See Summer days count all their mystic hours
By rhythmic pulses of perfecting life
Slow ripening toward fulfilment, — see them slip
Through Music's trances, through her voiceful
     bowers
In long-drawn dreams of marvellous delight.
Down yonder immemorial mountain gray
Night trails her unwilling splendors, loath to go;
Far o'er her cloudy home the mother Moon
Walketh the silence with one baby star
Still tugging at her skirt (a wondrous star,
The loveliest scion of her golden race);
And yet her mother-love with wider gaze
Holds in its large-eyed care the sleeping world.

The Soul that thrills my being's finest chord
Is never sight or sound I hear or see,
Albeit it touches me through everything;
But in that silence deeper than all speech,
Finer than utterance can ever be,
It moves my heart — it speaks with me.
This freckled field, with crests of plumy grain
Nodding before me all the afternoon,
And idly gossiping with idle gales,
Heedless of fruitage quickening at its heart;
Low-lying meadows, twinkling in the heats
Of harvest twilights; and the restless trees,
Tossing aspiring arms, with mighty moans
For freedom, giants of longing, bound
Forever, rooted in the earth's low heart,
Whose lifted faces front the eternal calm;
The ample heavens, the interfusing hills,
The silver runlet with its thread-like song
Lapsing to silence, and the psychal flowers
Whose subtle souls tell o'er the story of
Our human life; the myriad insect folk,
Stirring air-pulses with their ecstasy, —
All touch departed days, and I see thee.
The Indian Summer, the dead Summer's soul,

Comes back with more than the first loveliness, —
The all I've lost, the more I never found
Haunting her beauty, while for me she weaves
Of color, odor, sound, her perfect days.
Oh, brief as fair is her exquisite life!
And thus a sadness in the season's soul,
Touches the soul within me.   See, to-day
Her misty banner trembles on the hills!
The world lies floating in her nebulous gold;
Her low unrest, at once delight and pain,
Makes its delicious trouble in my breast.
The marvellous beauty that mine eyes can see;
The unimagined beauty that no sense
Can reach; the beauty that I dream of, yet
To be revealed in life's reality, —
Do all touch thee.   Fine, visible forms,
The invisible spirit of all loveliest things,
Heroic types of all things fair and best
Give back, and in my love transfigure thee,
Sole Love, my only Love.   Thus, I have learned
How one rare presence may fill all this world,
And that one presence be the world to me.

SONG.

UNDERNEATH the ample heaven,
　　While its sunshine flowed like wine,
While the pulse of life was thrilling,
　　In the Summer's spell divine,
When we stood alone with Nature,
　　Then thou wert wholly mine.

When the world of men shall claim us,
　　Where the lights of fashion shine;
When our souls no longer tremble
　　Unto tones so clear and fine,
When the idler's words allure thee,
　　Shall I alone be thine?

GOOD-NIGHT.

GOOD-NIGHT, my Love; I lay me down,
    The while the old clock of the town
Rings out for me a deep good-night.
Thou canst not hear the words I say,
Nor hear the tender prayer I pray,
That thou mayest love me sundered wide
As thou dost love me by thy side;
And so to thee, my heart's delight,
I say again love's last good-night.

Good-night. I 'm wondering how 't will be
When life is slipping far from me,
When, drawn by Death's tranquillity,
The far-off, fadeless morn I see.
Then wilt thou kiss the fading face,
So dear to thee in earlier grace?
And say: "No soul can take the place
Thy life-long love for thee hath won!

Good-night.   A little further on
I 'll take thy hand, I 'll kiss thine eyes,
Lit by the new life's rapt surprise.
The twin of soul, the truly wed,
Can never part.   Rest, wifely head !
Dear heart, be not disquieted ;
For fast I follow after thee,
To find Love's last reality ! "

Or shall I see but empty space
When mine eyes, dying, seek thy face ?
And wilt thou be too far from me
To hear my last good-night to thee ?
I know not.   Only this I know,
" Good-night," 't is sweet to murmur low.
By two dear words I 'm nearer thee, —
By all their priceless legacy,
And burden fond of memory
That holds thy first good-night to me.
Then music, thrilled with deeper tone,
Told but one story — true love's own ;
And life, *our life*, was just begun, —
Its meaning learned, two lives in one.

Good-night, dear Love!   I pray the Lord,
By every promise of his Word,
That, day and night, may follow thee,
With ever-folding ministry,
Thy better angels, holding thee
In all loud day's prosperity,
And in the haunting night-watch lone;
From all the evil sin hath wrought,
From tempting deed and soiling thought,
From sorrow and from murdered faith,
From loss in life and loss in death,
The blessèd angels hold thee sure,
And lead thee safe and save thee pure.

Good-night.   The old clock of the town
Strikes night's last hour.   The morning's crown
Touches the silence.   Dropping down,
Before 't is gone, the midnight quite,
Once more, O Love, a dear Good-night.

FAREWELL.

"FAREWELL," she said, her voice was low;
   "Farewell! To-morrow's sun will rise
To light thee where thy feet will go,
   Beneath far Southern skies."

"Farewell!" he said, in accents clear;
   "Farewell, — the mills of truth move slow
To prove to thee that thou wert dear,
   Dearer than thou didst know."

Farewell! farewell! Four tear-blind eyes,
   Two clasping hands that part so slow;
'T is hidden in God's mysteries,
   Why separate ways they go.

Farewell! Farewell! Through keen delights
 It strikes two hearts, this word of woe.
Through every joy of life it smites, —
 Why, sometime, they will know.

Farewell! The lonely word that parts
 Binds two in silence ever fast;
Each throbs to each, these sundered hearts,
 One in the sacred past.

INJUNCTION.

GO, thou good angel, in this night,
　　Through all its spaces long and dim,
Bear thou my traveller in his flight,
　　Safely from danger carry him!

Go, thou good angel, I must stay;
　　Helpless is love, in all its might,
When alien fate doth bear away
　　The best belovèd from our sight.

Touch, with thy talisman, the road,
　　To lessen evil, soften fate;
Thou only, of the sons of God,
　　Hast never lost thine high estate.

" I give my certain angels charge
  To hold for me life's lowliest waif,"
The Father saith; " Heaven is large,
  My love is sure, thy Love is safe."

Go, thou good angel, follow him !
  He speeds beyond mine outreached arms;
In earth's dire places, lone and dim,
  Hold him invincible to harms.

Come soon, dear angel, come and say :
  " Smile, saddest eyes, — thy flowers tend,
Thy tasks pursue; thy traveller's way
  I held in safety to the end."

Above the hills, beside the sea,
  Go, blessèd one, — mine eyes are dim;
Go, bring him safely back to me,
  Or bear me swiftly forth to him.

INTERROGATION.

O TINY leaflet, turning to the sun,
    What dost thou say?
Of tales thou tellest all — the sweetest one
    Tell me to-day?

Thou tender dawn, trembling upon the blue
    In bloom of pink,
Whisper the word I want; O whisper true
    The thing I think!

And thou, Arbutus, firstling of the May,
    In ruddy shoon,
Say, did my Lover ever come thy way
    By light of moon?

Or in the morning when the virgin dew
        Was on thy face,
Whose name above thy sweetness slowly grew
        In tone of grace?

Didst thou allure from him, O wooing pine,
        In accents clear,
His sacred secret, sealed from outward sign,
        That owned me dear?

Wind of the West! with budding willow-scent
        Thou bearest fleet —
With breath of clover, deep with dew besprent,
        Bring tidings sweet!

Alone with Nature, did his guarded lip,
        In phrase divine,
Do reverence to the wondrous fellowship —
        All his and mine?

NATURE.

NATURE.

———◆◇◆———

THANKSGIVING.

FALLING from yonder heaven of blue,
    God's blessing, healing as the dew,
Makes all my being blossom new.

I cannot see the world is fair,
Nor feel the sunshine, breathe the air,
Nor live, and not make life a prayer, —

A prayer of praise, a glad All-hail,
That drowneth every human wail,
In soaring up through Mercy's pale.

No phantasy of dazzling deed,
No cramping cincture of a creed,
Can fill with calm our deeper need.

I gaze beyond each sphered star;
I rise, through yonder calm afar,
To where my Father's mansions are.

I have no tear, no note forlorn,
For you, sweet breezes of the morn, —
I'm glad to-day that I was born.

I have a lover's kiss for you,
Rath violets, — rimmed with balmy dew,
From moss-weft covert peering through.

I bare my forehead to the sky;
And life's full fountain fills so high,
To breathe, to live, is ecstasy.

The nectar of all vanished Springs
This Spring from her new censer flings,
Thrills with new life all living things.

Come in, soft sunshine of the day, —
Serene, soft sunshine, God's own ray, —
To brighten all my upward way!

ARBUTUS.

DEAR, dear Arbutus, — thou dost bring
    Far more to me than tint of Spring,
More than her far and faint perfume
Into this dim and dusty room;
We are old friends, Arbutus; so
I saw thee smiling long ago.
Where is the child that culled and sung?
Afar I see her, fair and young.

Unto the woman's pleading touch
Yields the old sweetness — this is much;
All that thou gavest to me then —
And how much more — thou givest again!
This April morn thou art the same
As when unto the child thou came;
The shadow life hath o'er me flung
Doth reach thee not, O sweet and young!

Our love and sorrow mutely trace
The lines of life upon the face;
But deeper in the soul do write
All they have wrought afar from sight.
The rose of youth, its fadeless grace,
Liveth alone on Nature's face.

Thus, dear Arbutus, thou dost bring
Far more to me than tint of Spring, —
Than hint of far-off bursting brooks,
Of woody banks and noiseless nooks,
Where thy shy sisters hide and peer˙
Through leafy veils, with smile and tear,
The coyest coquettes of the year.

Mid din of street and rush of men
Thou makest all earth young again;
Thou sayest: " Far from men and mart
Still yearns thy mighty mother's heart;
She sends thee me thy heart to move,
Fresh token of her changeless love;
She says: ' Come back, O life-worn child!
Drink from my springs the undefiled ! '

" Deep, deep within my solitudes,
The soul of peace and soothing broods,
Half silent, all with life astir;
The morning murmur of the fir,
At dawn's high calm above the hill;
The threadlike ripple of the rill,
Lapsing through mosses fringing cool;
The stillness of the lilied pool;
The calmness of the mountain crown,
Poising a star the night drops down;
The rhythm of the awful sea,
Rolling from out eternity,
Calling, calling, eternally!

" Till thou, beyond the ocean's bar,
Beyond the gleam of sun or star,
Do seem to feel the Soul from far,
From whom it rolls, from whom we are,
The while the long, long tides bear in
Treasure and wreck, with muffled din, —
Then break in music's pulsing thrill
Along the sands when winds are still.

" When thou, poor soul, hast had thy fill
Of swift, loud life, — yet yearning still
For all thou hast not, bliss unfound,
Beyond thy speech or being's bound, —
Turn thou unto thy first love's grace;
Come, thou, and lay thy faded face
Upon my bosom.   Thou wilt see
That all that never faileth thee,
Abiding ever, changing not
With any chance of mortal lot,
Or any coldness of the heart,
Beyond the ken of human art,
Beyond all human power to give,
Deep in the universe do live,
Nor change nor death can them destroy,
The youth of Nature, Nature's joy."

Arbutus, thou dost faintly swing
The subtle censer of the Spring.
I sip thy wine, I kiss thy lips,
I softly touch thy pinky tips.
More than I say, art thou to me, —
A past and still a joy to be!

If e'er I stand of all bereft,
As they do stand whom Death has left,
A treasure dearer far than gold
Mine empty hands will seek and hold, —
The first Arbutus of the Spring.
A simple thing, a little thing,
Yet incense-bearer to the King,
His tidings glad borne on its wing.
All my lost life 't will backward bring,
And all the life before 't will touch
With Spring's young glory.   'T will be **much** —
How much!   Yet such a little thing,
The first Arbutus of the Spring!

THE SEED.

O WINGÈD seed from June's rich zone,
 Borne with delicious monotone
To me, come in. I'm all alone.
Come in, come in! My world is dry;
From wearying work I turn and sigh
With yearning for the far, free sky.
No limit binds its wondrous tent
Whose boundless blue is o'er me bent.
Out of the hot street's boisterous din,
O wingèd seed, come in, come in!

Rover from Nature's kingdom, when
Didst think to come to that of men?
Dear little seed, how good of thee
To leave the All and come to me.
How couldst thou? Fair the realm I see
Where thou wert born. There all are free,—
The tiny people of the ground,
Who live and love and brood and bear;

The murmuring people of the air,
Who thrill vast silence into sound;
Thy mother flower, whose final dower
Was thee — seed of her primal hour;
Loosed from her heart without a sound,
Thou comest to a prisoner bound.

A prisoner within these walls,
While every sound of Nature calls
Me from the meagre strife of men.
I may not go.   In pity, then,
She quickened thee, mysterious seed,
And sent thee to me in my need.

Through parting gates of bending grass,
O spirit seed, I see thee pass,
And, sailing on the deep, still air,
Still on thy subtle message bear.
What flowers wooed on myriad slopes,
What birds sang out their loves and hopes,
What longing called in tender leaves,
That murmured through the morns and eves!
No one could lure thee, wingèd seed;
To me thou comest in my need.

What is thy message from my Lord?
Give me the gospel of thy word!
Is 't this? " Thy heart is slow to grant
Largess to toil, and slow to plant
In shallow furrows tiny seed
Thy Master gives thee. Thou dost heed
The songs that haunt the Summer day,
And pause to hear from far away,
On mountain top, the lofty strain
That is not thine. 'T is thine in pain
And sorrow often to drop low
A little seed that may not grow
At all; and yet, some blessèd day,
Another, falling by the way
From thy tired hand, may spring and bloom,
And cast its seed to find sweet room
In some sad, waiting human soul —
As I this morn have found my goal,
And sent my quickening thrill through thine,
To breathe and bear a fruit divine.
A million perished by the way
Ere I could reach thy heart to-day."

A PERFECT DAY.

GO, glorious day!
    Here, while you pass, I make this sign:
Earth, swinging on her silent way,
    Will bear me back unto this hour divine,
    And I will softly say: "Once thou wert mine.

"Wert mine, O perfect day!
    The light unknown, soaring from sea and shore,
The forest's eager blaze,
    The flaming torches that the Autumn bore,
    The fusing sunset seas when storms were o'er:

"Were mine the brooding airs,
    The pulsing music of the weedy brooks,
The jewelled fishes and the mossy lairs,
    Wherein shy creatures, with their free, bright
        looks,
    Taught blessèd lessons, never found in books:

" All mine the peace of God,
 When it was joy enough to breathe and be,
The peace of Nature oozing from her sod,
 When face to face with her the soul was free,
 And far the false, wild strife it fain would flee."

Stay, beauteous day!
 Yet why pray I? Thy lot, like mine, to fade.
Thy light, like yonder mountain's golden haze,
 Must merge into the morrow's misty shade;
And I, an exile in the alien street,
Still gazing back, yearn toward the vision fleet.

" Once thou wert mine!" I 'll say,
 And comfort so my heart, as with old wine.
Poor pilgrims! oft we walk the self-same way,
 To weep its change, to kneel before the shrine
The heart once builded to a happy day,
 When dear it died. I 'll say: "O day divine,
  Life presses sore; but once, *once* thou wert
   mine."

THE MOUNTAIN PINE.

A FAR within the fainting town,
    Where waves of heat come rolling
        down,
    And men sink down to die,
I seemed to drink thy wine divine,
I saw thy face, O mountain pine,
    And yet could not draw nigh.

I said: "The breath of heaven is sweet,
And balm and peace and silence meet
    Upon the lonely hill.
Hush, weary heart. Thou soon wilt find
The even pulse, the rested mind,
    In regions cool and still.

"The pulses of my life run low,
Effort is feeble, purpose slow,
  'Why strive?' you sadly say.
Wait! Thou shalt taste the saving wine,
Poured for thee by the mountain pine,
  Some later Summer day.

"Afar for thee the mountain pine
Distils the odor of its wine
  And fills its chalice up,
And waits through dewy morning's calm,
Through stilly evening's brooding balm,
  To fill thine eager cup."

I saw it through the twilight dim,
I heard the murmur of its hymn
  Above the noisy street;
I said: "Press deep, ye thorns of fate,
Your wounds will heal, and I can wait
  The balsam strong and sweet."

Lo, here am I. O mountain pine,
Pour for the pilgrim of thy wine,
  Then fill thy chalice up;
Again and yet again I 'll stand;
Again and yet again thy hand
  Will fill my empty cup.

The world that I have left behind
Has drained the fountains of the mind
  And sapped the weakened will.
O mother earth, from out the strife
I come to thee for life, for life,
  And here I drink my fill.

I sit beneath the mountain pine,
I press its fingers small and fine,
  I taste its honeyed cone.
And downward, from the glimmering skies,
Come flocks of flickering butterflies,
  And I am not alone.

Out from the softly woven thread
Of the brown carpet, round me spread,
   Come creatures clean and small;
Each happy in its bright, brief day,
Perfect in every work and way,
   To me it seems to call.

It says: "On the eternal leaf
The measure of thy day is brief,
   A fragment but as mine.
Thou beatest in thy little space,
Yet cannot more than fill thy place
   Within the plan divine.

"Why chafe within thy narrow range?
Why sigh that life must change and change?
   Why weep o'er love's dear cost?
Thy failure and thy want shall still
The purpose of thy life fulfil,
   And nothing can be lost.

" The wrong that thou hast borne may give
Thee strength to help another live ;
   The tear, that falls apart,
May thrill with human tenderness
The unconscious word you breathe, to bless
   Some aching human heart.

" Take without question life's great gift,
Its love, its pain, its toil, its shrift,
   Its never-rounded arc ;
For when the body's day is spent,
Transmuted, through each element,
   'T will live, Life's endless spark."

I sit beneath thee, mountain pine, —
I breathe thy balm, I drink thy wine, —
   Upon the lonely hill.
The world lies far beneath my feet ;
Again my life is strong and sweet,
   In regions high and still.

I listen to the longed-for hymn,
Chanted within thine arches dim,
  Far up the azure air.
Ye subtle murmurs, floating o'er
From some far, spiritual shore,
  What messages ye bear!

What hints of high, immortal things
Come floating down on unseen wings,
  To thrill the heart of care,
To reassure the fainting mind,
That saddens, lest it cannot find
  Worlds that are still more fair!

Ah, when the restless city street
Again receives my rested feet,
  I 'll lift my vested wine;
I 'll listen, in my chamber dim,
The low chant of thy far-off hymn,
  O sacred mountain pine.

And when the springs of life run low,
Effort grows feeble, purpose slow,
   Fill, fill thy chalice up.
Again and yet again I 'll stand;
Again and yet again thy hand
   Shall fill my empty cup.

CATSKILL MOUNTAINS, September, 1876.

AN OCTOBER IDYL.

ON the scarlet mountains yonder,
　　Summer lies down to die;
She gathers her robes of splendor
　　Around her royally.
Her minions, the lowly grasses,
　　Are weeping about her bed,
And her gentle maiden-mosses
　　Pillow her dying head.

She was cruel in her splendor,
　　She mocked us in her reign;
She held her careless carnival
　　Above our idol slain.
It failed, the precious promise
　　Of her glory's dawning reign;
They came, the loss and the longing,
　　The silence and the pain.

For 't is not the hand that crowns us,
   The hand held out to bless;
'T is the hand that wrongs and wounds us,
   That we oftenest caress.
Thus, O thou beguiling Summer,
   We o'er thy beauty lean.
Thou didst rob us, yet we love thee;
   Thou art dying, O our Queen!

All passionate fervor faded, –
   With eyes, at last serene,
Turned to thy conqueror, Autumn,
   Thou art dying, still our Queen!
All thou didst give unto us,
   In thy morning's gracious glow,
And all thou had taken from us,
   Only our God can know.

GOLDEN-ROD.

I'VE reached the land of Golden-rod,
   Afar I see it wave and nod.
But yesterday in fiery street
I heard the tramp of tired feet;
Now, on the heart of August noon,
Wood-waters lapse in rippling tune.
The curtains of the mossy burn
Wear fringes deep of fragrant fern;
The arches of its shining sluice
Are slender spirals of the spruce.
While far above I see them stir
The lances of the stately fir,
And on the down — I see it nod
And beckon me — the Golden-rod.

But yesterday it seemed to me
That I could never turn and flee,
Or ever find that quiet spot
Where greed and gain and noise are not.

How far away the vexing strife,
The turmoil sad, men misname life!
Now here I wait till sunset dyes
Steal through the azure of the skies,
And soaring hill and circling plain
Flush radiant with their rosy stain.

I wait till twilight, brooding deep,
Takes earth within her arms asleep,
And only low half-tones are heard:
The flutter of the dreaming bird;
The brooklet's rune below the pine;
Low-leaping trout that spring and shine;
The squirrel's rustle by the road;
The farm-horse bearing home his load;
The patter of the dropping burr;
Grasshoppers in their holes astir;
The cricket and the katydid
Calling, in leafy houses hid;
The bleat of lambs upon the hill;
The cow-boy calling, keen and shrill;
The cow-bells' answering, tinkling trill;
The murmurs of a world at peace,
That stir and thrill and softly cease.

O peaceful realm of Golden-rod!
O kingdom of the clovery sod!
Thy tiny people of the ground
Do reign devoid of jarring sound.
Thy happy nations of the air
Fulfil their fate, all free of care;
They carry into God's good plan
None of the loud ado of man.
How far the thunder of the mart,
The wear and tear and wound and smart:
Ambition's war, the greed of gain,
The lust of power; faith slowly slain;
Man thrusting man on Failure's wall;
Man rising on his brother's fall;
The rush for prizes never earned;
The show of wisdom never learned;
The poor pretence; the flowery snare
That kills a soul, yet seems so fair;
Love wounded daily till it dies;
The heart bereft, that inly sighs;
The loneliness; the sense of loss,
Of treasure missed, the human cross
That every living soul must bear;
What wonder that it seems so fair

Beside man's weary world of sin,
Thy world, that no sin enters in —
O kingdom of the clovery sod,
O peaceful realm of Golden-rod!

I pluck the Milk-weed's pallid pod,
And set it with the Golden-rod;
I tarry long, I linger late,
I cry: "O world of work await;
I cannot hasten unto thee.
In Nature's kingdom I am free —
Free from the worker's ceaseless strain,
Tasks never done; the low, dull pain,
Piercing the over-burdened brain!
O weary world of work, await,
Nor call me from my high estate "

Yonder, between two mountains vast,
The bright shield of the lake is cast.
O splendor of the far, deep sky,
Of mountain soaring lone and high,
Of lake that flashes at its feet,
Of ferns and mosses cool and sweet;
O beauty brooding everywhere,

The essence of the earth and air,
The ringing brook, the pool's still well,
The sunlit slope, the shaded dell, —
How can I say to you, Farewell?

I lie amid the Golden-rod,
I love to see it lean and nod;
I love to feel the grassy sod
Whose kindly breast will hold me last,
Whose patient arms will fold me fast —
Fold me from sunshine and from song,
Fold me from sorrow and from wrong.
Through gleaming gates of Golden-rod
I 'll pass into the rest of God.

NANTASKET.

FAIR is thy face, Nantasket,
  And fair thy curving shores;
The peering spires of villages;
  The boatman's dipping oars;
The lonely ledge of Minot,
  Where the watchman tends his light,
And sets its perilous beacon —
  A star in the stormiest night.

Along thy vast sea highways
  The great ships slide from sight,
And flocks of wingèd phantoms
  Flit by like birds in flight.

Over the toppling sea-wall
  The homebound dories float;
I see the patient fisherman
  Bend in his anchored boat.

I am alone with Nature,
  With the soft September day;
The lifting hills above me,
  With golden-rod are gay.
Across the fields of ether
  Flit butterflies at play;
And cones of garnet sumach
  Glow down the country way.

The Autumn dandelion
  Beside the roadside burns;
Above the lichened bowlders
  Quiver the plumèd ferns.
The cream-white silk of the milkweed
  Floats from its sea-green pod;
From out the mossy rock-seams
  Flashes the golden-rod.

The woodbine's scarlet banners
   Flaunt from their towers of stone;
The wan, wild morning-glory
   Dies by the road alone.
By the hill-path to the seaside
   Wave myriad azure bells;
Over the grassy ramparts
   Bend milky immortelles.

Within the sea-washed meadow
   The wild grape climbs the wall;
From off the o'er-ripe chestnuts
   The brown burrs softly fall;
I hear in the woods of Hingham
   The mellow caw of the crow,
Till I seem in the woods of Wachuset
   In August's sumptuous glow.

I see late daisies leaning
   Along the wayside bars;
The tangled green of the thicket
   Glows with the aster's stars;

Beside the brook the gentian
  Closes its fringèd eyes,
And waits the enticing glory
  Of October's yellow skies.

The tiny boom of the beetle
  Smites the shining rocks below;
The gauzy oar of the dragon-fly
  Is beating to and fro;
The lovely ghost of the thistle
  Goes sailing softly by;
Glad in its second Summer
  Hums the awakened fly.

I see the tall reeds shiver
  Beside the salt sea marge;
I see the seabird glimmer
  Far out on airy barge.
The cumulate cry of the cricket
  Pierces the amber noon;
Over and through it Ocean
  Chants his pervasive rune.

Fair is the earth behind me,
  Vast is the sea before;
Afar in the misty mirage
  Glistens another shore.
Is it a realm enchanted?
  It cannot be more fair
Than this nook of Nature's kingdom,
  With its spell of space and air.

Lo, over the sapphire ocean
  Trembles a bridge of flame, —
To the burning core of the sunset,
  To the city too fair to name;
Till a ray of its inner glory
  Streams to this lower sea,
And we see with human vision
  What Heaven itself may be.

AN OCTOBER PICTURE.

OUT of the great sun's sinking crest
　　Drop myriad stars on the river's breast.

The mountains glow like amethysts
Through filmy veils of yellow mists.

Their purple and amber, blazoned near,
Warm the autumn ether, crystal clear.

The wonderful light of the fading day
Is full of the perfume of late-mown hay.

Its glory falls on the fragrant wains,
Rolling home through the ferny lanes.

The lowly homestead, brown and old,
Spreadeth above us a roof of gold.

We run about 'neath its sheltering eaves,
And weave our wreaths of the fallen leaves.

To and fro we cross and pass,
While the cricket cries in the russet grass.

We hear, mid our play in the wood on the hill,
The lonely call of the whip-poor-will,

And the answering caw of the mocking crow,
Taunting poor Will's melodious woe.

The squirrels scamper from out their lairs,
And run with nuts up the tall tree-stairs.

We hold our hats 'neath its loaded crown,
And the old tree drops its chestnuts down.

We burrow deep in the earthworn ruts
For the velvet-coated butternuts.

The falchioned ferns still swing and nod,
Marshalling hosts of the golden-rod.

Above the tremulous asters lean;
Below the primrose prays unseen.

The holy twilight, sweet and long,
Is full of the children's shout and song.

The twilight dies, the stars arise, —
Night awes us not with mysteries;

For yet, in our unasking eyes,
God's miracles wake no surprise.

Never a grief hath made us weep,
Too deep for our mother's heart to keep.

We are children — the gauds of sin,
Of gain, of ambition, yet to win.

We are children — unlearned the art
That will lead us far from nature's heart.

No cross of life can make us sigh;
No baffling fate to solve we try.

We take the gifts of earth and sky,
The largess of love, and know not why.

Serene as October's sunset skies,
The land of childhood about us lies.

———

Here in the city's dust I see
This far-off picture dear to me;

I hang it up, mid beating rains, —
" Children at play in October Lanes," —

And watch for the Hand that will lead me hence,
Out to the land of Innocence.

HAPPY DAYS.

STAY, happy days! Why will ye go?
　　Forever I would keep your glow;
The light hid in your mystic strand
Was never seen on sea or land.

All shut within your shining ray
The auras of your mystery play;
The spell of human joy ye hold,
A spring within your heart of gold.

It leaps in yon vast sea of blue
That emerald fields of earth bedew;
Deep in the forest pine 't is pent,
The youth and health of fragrant scent.

A sinuous river softly streams,
Beyond the opal ocean gleams;
The placid valleys tranquil bear
The nebula of amber air.

I watch sun-arrows softly fall
Aslant along the pine-arched wall;
I pluck within my fern-fringed nook
The scarlet berries by the brook.

Low in the boughs above my head
I hear the stir of robin red,
And musing on a shady knoll
I see a lingering oriole.

Nut-laden from the mossy deeps
The quick-eyed squirrel swiftly leaps;
Beneath his panoply of shade
The dainty hare sits un-afraid.

The partridge beats his slender drum;
In roadside thicket insects hum;
Within the grass shrill crickets cry;
Idly flaunts by the butterfly.

And all the golden space is stirred
By glancing oar of humming-bird,
While in the sun the belted bee,
Gay minstrel, stings the air with glee.

Close clinging down the clovery strath
I see wisps sweet of after-math;
And all the blue above me bent
Is full of leisure and content.

The morning splendor could not last.
The noon's apocalypse is past;
The glory of the day is gone —
The after-glow burns softly on.

Earth's monotones, so sweet and sad,
Deep thrill the heart — half make it glad;
What benison of beauty lies
In yon deep peace of twilight skies,

Stay happy day! The throb of life
Hath lost the fever of its strife;
From stress and hurt we find release
In Nature's soothing, in her peace.

O happy Soul of happy days, —
Our Father's Love! its countless rays
Fall in His all-pervading thought,
In all the earth's vast beauty wrought.

INTERVALE, N. H., 1882.

RELIGION.

RELIGION.

—◦—

ALONE WITH GOD.

ALONE with God! Day's craven cares
Have crowded onward, unawares.
The soul is left to breathe her prayers.

Alone with God! I bare my breast;
Come in, come in, O Holy Guest,
Give rest, Thy rest, — of rest the best!

Alone with God! How deep a calm
Steals o'er me, — sweet as music's balm,
When seraphs sing a seraph's psalm.

Alone with God! No human eye
Is here, with eager look, to pry
Into the meaning of each sigh.

Alone with God! No jealous glare
Now stings me with its torturing stare;
No human malice says Beware!

Alone with God! From earth's rude crowd,
With jostling steps and laughter loud,
My better soul I need not shroud.

Alone with God! He only knows,
If sorrow's ocean overflows,
The silent spring from whence it rose.

Alone with God! He mercy lends.
Life's fainting hope, life's meagre ends,
Life's dwarfing pain, He comprehends.

Alone with God! He feeleth well
The soul's pent life that will o'erswell,
The lifelong want no words may tell.

Alone with God! Still nearer bend,
O tender Father; condescend,
In this my need, to be my friend.

Alone with God! With suppliant mien,
Upon Thy pitying breast I lean,—
No less because Thou art unseen.

Alone with God! Safe in Thy arms,
O shield me from life's wild alarms!
O save me from life's fearful harms!

Alone with God! Oh sweet to me
This cover, to whose shades I flee,
To breathe repose in Thee, in Thee.

A WOMAN'S HYMN TO CHRIST.

JESUS WEPT! This thought returning
To my soul, forever yearning,
Stills its sobbing, stays its burning.

Jesus wept! The God-power keeping —
There, where Lazarus lay sleeping,
Wept the man, with women weeping.

Jesus wept! A God's compassion, —
Ruth, no human soul can fashion,
From its sin-born pain or passion.

Jesus wept! Prayers flow the faster;
Is it strange still woman casts her
Care on thee, O Jesu, Master?

Thou whose love doth so defend her;
Thou whose word such hope can lend her,
Sacred, saving, soothing, tender!

Ah, Thou knowest, if forgiven
She, in tears and pain, hath striven
Since the hour from Eden driven!

Men were ready to deride her;
To Thy breast she turned to hide her, —
Sure of shelter else denied her.

Thou knewest souls would ne'er be wanting
Who would bless this woman, pointing
Unto hers, Love's last anointing!

Men — all eager to disown her —
Brought the fallen; they would stone her.
"Daughter!" Thou saidst; Thou couldst own
     her.

Sin its ceaseless strife still wages;
Souls are sinking, passion rages;
Woman calls Thee through the ages.

Gone, Thou art, — yet low she falleth;
Unto Thee she calleth, calleth,
For the love which never palleth.

All unseen Thy heart gives heeding
To thy poor child's piteous pleading;
Thou dost lift the bowed, the bleeding!

Soft low couch for sleep, Thou 'lt make her;
In the morn Thy voice shall wake her;
To Thy bosom Thou wilt take her.

WAITING.

I WAIT,
   Till from my veilèd brows shall fall
This baffling cloud, this wearying thrall,
Which holds me now from knowing all;
Until my spirit sight shall see
Into all Being's mystery,
See what it really is to be!

   I wait,
While robbing days in mockery fling
Such cruel loss athwart my Spring,
And life flags on with broken wing;
Believing that a kindlier fate
The patient soul will compensate
For all it loses, ere too late.

I wait!
For surely every scanty seed,
I plant in weakness and in need,
Will blossom in perfected deed!
Mine eyes shall see its affluent crown,
Its fragrant fruitage, dropping down
Care's lowly levels, bare and brown!

I wait,
Till in white Death's tranquillity,
Shall softly fall away from me,
This weary life's infirmity;
That I, in larger light, may learn
The larger truth I would discern,
The larger love for which I yearn.

I wait!
The Summer of the soul is long,
Its harvests yet shall round me throng,
In perfect pomp of sun and song.
In stormless mornings, yet to be,
I'll pluck, from life's full-fruited tree,
The joy to-day denied to me.

SABBATH VERSES.

IN holy rest, this Sabbath day,
    Blue gleam the waters of the bay,
While out upon the lullèd deep
The resting winds lie fast asleep.

And, floating on the drooping gales,
The sea-gull waves its weary sails;
The little waves, with eager lips,
Run up and kiss the sleeping ships.

Along the upper azure sea,
Clouds sail in soft serenity,
And line the far horizon's rim
With tranquil islands violet-dim.

The air is fraught with worship's balm,
And full of love's seraphic calm;
Lord, smiling through its Sabbath trance,
How fair is Thy day's countenance!

Dear Lord! dost weary of the plaints,
The tears and sighings of Thy saints?
For, ever since the Eden fall,
Hath life been one long cry and call.

For sorrow comes of sin; and so
Thy children pray, while centuries go,
That Thou wilt show their tearful eyes
The lovely lands of Paradise.

But mists of fear bedim the day,
And dark and doubtful seems the way;
O help us o'er the abyss of fate,
And lead us back to Eden's gate!

Our human life is one vast need;
We sigh to know to-morrow's meed,
And, yearning, seek to comprehend
The why of Being and its end!

For every pang of soul or sense,
'T would be the richest recompense
To know the joy that is to be,
To see the life we cannot see!

Thy ways are past our finding out;
We walk in mystery and in doubt.
Dear Lord, outstretch Thy patient hand,
And lead us till we understand.

From burdened brows before Thee bent
Smooth all the lines of discontent;
Let longing heart and aching head
Rest on Thy bosom, comforted.

And when the tired soul shall faint,
O weary not of its complaint;
But lift us to the Shining Gates,
And show us where fruition waits.

REST.

HE prayed alone, our Lord most dear:
 The men who loved him fell fast asleep;
His tender cry they did not hear;
 His watch one hour they could not keep.

His soul was sorrowful unto death.
 " Tarry ye here and watch with me,"
Cried his yearning heart, his pleading breath.
 Their eyes were heavy, they did not see.

Their sight was sealed from the God-man's face;
 His piteous human life was done.
Dear was it, Lord, — its haunting grace,
 Its loves withheld, its heights unwon?

Or was thine anguish all for men,
　　The sad, ungrateful, graceless race
Thou cam'st to save, — who, in thy pain,
　　Alas, did not discern thy face?

"The hour 's at hand when the Son of Man
　　Shall be betrayed," thy lips confest;
"My need is done! Lo, now ye can
　　Sleep on, sleep on, and take your rest!"

　　.　　.　　.　　.　　.

Some day from our tired hands will fall
　　Our half-done tasks. Then sore opprest
Will be the soul, till it hear the call:
　　"Dear heart, sleep now, and take thy rest."

All love, all loss, all longing done, —
　　Ah, then what boon will be the best
To the vanquished soul, its worlds unwon?
　　"Sleep now in peace, and take thy rest."

Beneath fulfilment we miss so much, —
　　Hopes unallowed, love unconfest;
Each life must miss the consummate touch
　　That could make it perfect, crown it blest;

But it floweth still, from the inmost sphere,
    For thee, for me, that soft behest,
Touched with the God-man's tenderest tear:
    " Sleep now, tired heart, and take thy rest."

Dear Lord, amid thy Seraphim,
    Dost thou remember how all alone
Thou wert on earth in that garden dim,
    When thy nearest friends heard not thy moan?

Human! Alone! Doth thy shining face
    Grow sad at thought of that grief unblest?
I hear: " Poor child of a fallen race,
    Sleep now, sleep now, and take thy rest."

To-day our Lord, on his steadfast throne,
    Let us forget not, loves us still, —
Pities, as when He wept alone,
    The weary of heart, the weak of will.

So when our striving all is done,
    And our hands are folded, — that will be best;
The much we have missed, the little won,
    Will be alike when in Him we rest.

      Easter, 1880.

AN OUTCAST.

WERE you once a baby fair?
    Did a mother's holy care
O'er thy helpless beauty wait?
Say she died, — nor dreamed thy fate.
Mother's baby once! and now
What a curse-mark on thy brow!
All the lovely body marred,
All the soul with sinning scarred.

Thine a fate as old as time, —
Lost, an outcast.   His the crime,
His the triumph; thine the pain,
Thine the anguish in the rain.
Never house-door opens wide,
Never pleasant voice inside
Says to thee: "Sad soul, come in;
Rest from roving, cease from sin."

Much I marvel while I see
Sister-women scorning thee, —
Sheltered women, whom love's care
Foldeth safe from every snare.
What hath made the difference
'Twixt thy sin, their innocence?
Would it be so fair and wide
Had they been as sorely tried?
Only He who made us knows
The real soul beneath its shows;
Only He will judge thee just
Who remembereth we are dust.
Day by day I marvel more
At each gilded dome and door
Builded, gilded, for the Lord;
At the spires pierced heavenward;
At the carven altars wide,
Thronged with pomp and praying pride,
While poor sinners stand outside.

Then the Lord himself I see
On the shores of Galilee,

A wayfarer by the road,
Bowed with more than mortal load.
O'er him soar no costly piles.
Through the cornfield's waving aisles
He the lowly people leads;
He the tired and hungry feeds;
And his grace outflows to them
Who but touch his garment's hem;
And his hand is outstretched free
To uplift such souls as thee!

What my right to pictured peace,
What my right to beauteous ease,
While outside my window pane
Walks an Outcast in the rain?
If for thee and me One died,
In his love we both abide;
All the love that saveth me
Reacheth out no less to thee.

Past the glance of human scorn,
Thank thy God that One was born

Who can save thee from thy fate,
Pure yet all-compassionate.
All the centuries are sweet
With his mercy.   It is meet
Thou shouldst call him o'er and o'er;
Still he answers: "Sin no more.
I forgive thee; sin no more."

THE CHRISTMAS CHRIST.

THIS is the morn, dear Lord, when Thou wert
    born,
And in its starry dawn no note forlorn
Paineth the silence. Joyous shouts instead
Fill the wide rooms from every little bed
Where wake the children. Larger children we,
Yet, Lord, Thy children love to sing to Thee
Our Christmas carol. All the blessèd morn
Is glad with bells that Thou, dear Lord, wert born.

We hang the holly for our walls to wear;
We braid its berries in our shining hair;
We garnish all our homes with fondest care;
We open wide our door, washed clean of sin,
That Thou, dear Christmas Christ, may'st enter in.
Upon its threshold say, beloved Guest:
" Peace be unto this house; I give it rest."

Abide with us, O Lord; go not away
When the bright scarlets of this Christmas day
Die in the West.   Then tarry with us still.
We 'll know Thou 'rt with us when thine eyes o'erfill
With pitying tears for all our suffering race.
With Thy compassion, give to us Thy grace, —
In our own frailty, grief for all who fall;
In our own need for loving, love for all
Who, through their empty days, for sweet love call.

Beneath the treasure-fruited trees
Thine, all, are these dear little children.   These
Are just as lovely, in their later glee,
As were the beauteous babes of Galilee,
Whose untouched innocence and loveliness
Thou, in Thy heavenly arms, didst bear and bless.
These little faces cannot see Thy face,
Nor feel the beauty of Thy human grace.
Oh, draw their dawning spirits nearer Thee,
Till, through Thy holy soul, their eyes shall see
Thy lovely countenance, — *Thyself*, discern:
So surely knowing, loving Thee, shall learn
To build their earthly days in shape like Thine,
Through human need to reach the fruit divine.

Dear Christmas Christ, come very near to her,
The childless mother.   Be her comforter!
To her the empty house is all too still:
No little stockings for her love to fill,
No cluster fair of shining little heads;
No rosy little forms in trundle-beds;
Her empty hands can only gather fast
The lonely playthings scattered in the past;
O Christus! give them back to her at last.

How fair, this Christmas morn, doth sunshine fall
On flowering capital, on azured wall,
On gleaming masses of yon pillared pile.
O Christmas Christ! thus may Thy constant smile
Fall on the people.   May Thy healing hand,
With touch of peace, lie on the eager land.
Thou, who didst cast the money-changers out
Of Thine own Temple, mid the selfish shout
And cry for power, come to this Capitol,
The people's Temple; banish from her hall
The money-changers, who, with jest and gibe,
Sell Truth and Honor.   From the touch of bribe
Wash each hand white.   Then every man will stand
True priest and prophet.   In its mighty band

The Nation's manhood, and its womanhood,
The welded will and conscience of the good,
On heights undreamed of yet, shall meet and mate,
And Truth and Honor, wedded, crown the State.

Again I hear the rapturous organ's chant;
And chorals quivering with human want
And human ecstasy ascend to Thee.
Beneath this cedared arch, this ivied fane,
O Christmas Christ, let us not pray in vain
For Thy poor creatures crying in their pain,
In Earth's dark places, where Thy face is not.
Amid the praises of our happier lot,
We pray for *them*.   Thy poor are everywhere;
And every one with less of love than care,
Whate'er of loss or longing be his share,
Feels human life a heavy load to bear.
The banners of the snow are wide unfurled,
And all inviolate the virgin world
In her white purity looks up to Thee,
O Love of love!   O deepest Mystery!
Thine own, own world, — Thy lovely earth-life died
For her dear sake.   To-day unsatisfied

She waits Thy coming.   Claim this hour Thy
    bride;
Rule over her, greater than all beside.
Through the vast eons of the far To Be,
May she find all things dear, in finding Thee;
All yearning stilled upon Thy sinless breast:
The world is Thine, O Master, give her rest.

LOSS AND GAIN.

EACH year's a robber, plucking, in its passing,
  Some priceless treasure we had set apart
To beautify all life, — the soul of pleasure,
  The sacred idol in the secret heart.
The robbing years! Aye, each one leaves us poorer,
  Seizing some love we hold at priceless cost:
All life seems empty — void one place forever;
  Mid treasure left, we weep the treasure lost.

Not wholly lost! I deem some far-off morning,
  Roaming in peace along Heaven's restful sward,
We'll come, all unaware, upon our treasures,
  All garnered for us by our loving Lord.
My friend I hold immortal in possession;
  Eternal is the " mine and thine; " away,
Ransomed from mortal life and death's oppression,
  We'll find the love we seem to lose to-day.

QUESTIONS.

CHRIST, from Thy birth-hour far and
  dim,
 In melodies that never cease,
Has Earth sung one perpetual hymn;
 Thy Kingdom, Lord, is full of peace.
Thy lovely seasons come and go;
 The Summer spreads her azure tent;
Her myriad flowers bud and blow;
 Her waving forests, light besprent,
Still woo us to their brooding calm,
 Still fill us with their deep content.

Their spicy balsams, healing balms,
 Exude their wine in every walk;
From garrulous dawn to even calms
 Do running rivulets laugh and talk.

They fill me with their dreamy tune,
    As by my window sail the bees;
And, sailing through the pomp of noon,
    Fair cloud-fleets throng the sapphire seas.

The cricket's chant is free of cares,
    Its slender pipe seems never dumb;
And all the amber August's airs
    Athrill with happy insect hum;
And flickers all the Summer's flame
    With humming-birds and butterflies;
Dear katydids seem half to blame,
    And half to praise, in tender cries.

The topaz glow above the hills,
    In which the harvest sun has set,
Is pure as gold that touched the rills,
    And lit the crown of Olivet.
The royal purple light that lies
    This evening on the silent sea,
Is rare as that that filled the skies,
    And flushed the waves of Galilee.

Long gazing toward the sacred sky,
   And outward o'er the clovery sward, —
"Earth is the same, unchanged," I cry,
   "But where art Thou, belovèd Lord?"
Where art Thou, Master? Long ago
   Thou lovedst Thy children, walked with
      them;
And healing, at the touch of woe,
   Fell from Thy very garment's hem.
Peace falling in Thy words of grace
   Made mourning mortal hearts rejoice;
Then they who loved Thee saw Thy face,
   And listened to Thy human voice.

I strain my eyes, yet cannot see;
   I lift my heart, nor dare believe
Thou 'lt bid all doubt and terror flee,
   Thou 'lt come to comfort when I grieve.
O draw the veil from off my eyes,
   O take the darkness from my heart!
Through mists of cloudy centuries,
   I would behold Thee as Thou art.

The hand I love may loose its hold,
 The heart I lean on most may fail;
Whose love but Thine can me enfold?
 Who else uphold when life shall pale?
O gentle heart! O tender eyes!
 O human love, my dearest meed!
And yet, what human love supplies
 The utmost measure of my need?

Baptized by Sorrow's awful chrism,
 Can mortal love our burden bear?
Alone in Being's dark abysm,
 We live the life no life may share.
No life save Thine, beloved Lord,
 Can fill its yearnings, heal its fret;
Tell me, while leaning on Thy Word,
 Thou art my heavenly kinsman yet.

LIGHT.

I 'VE sought Thee where the incense burned
    Beneath cathedral arches dim,
And high within the fabled Heaven,
    Enthroned above Thy seraphim.

I 've sought Thee through the blinding cloud
    Wherewith the creedsman hides Thy face;
All cold within the misty shroud
    It lacked for me the saving grace.

I put aside the veiling years,
    So baffling in their cloudy light.
And far above my blinding fears
    I seek to see thee, Lord, aright.

All safe from Doubt's uprising flood,
   I now with undimmed vision scan,
Not only grandeur of the God —
   Thy simple majesty as man.

What comfort to the souls that bleed
   Is cruel God, unknown, unseen;
But near in every human need,
   Doth come the Christ, the Nazarene.

O pilgrim in a lonely land,
   Who lonely wandered up and down;
Men followed, felt Thy healing hand,
   But no man ever saw Thy crown.

Thou gavest joy all men hold dear,
   The marvel of Thy gift to prove, —
The home that holds men safe from fear,
   The child's sweet grace, fair woman's love.

Thou givest now in dearth and loss
   Thy help, that we all good may gain,
Thy strength that bears another's cross,
   Thy love that soothes another's pain.

'T is not the thought that Jesus died
 That comfort to my heart doth give;
But, more than all the world beside,
 That evermore the Christ doth live.

TO AN INFIDEL.

L EAVE us Our Father! Lonely orphans we,
    Leave us the slender comfort of our faith;
Almighty Lover, whom we may not see,
    Lift us to life immortal up through death!

The mystic murmur of the Universe
    May croon of nothing. All the planets wheel,
Nerveless and aimless. All the floods rehearse
    Anthems of chance, no verity reveal.

Mutation's cruel hand forever rests
    On Nature, on our faces, on our lives;
Beyond our feeble will Fate works behests,
    Above our cry, our pain, Death binds his gyves.

Fragments are we, — fragment our meagre span!
   But as we faint and falter toward the dust,
Leave us our poem of the Immortal Man,
   Leave us Our Father whom we love and trust.

Leave us our vision.   On death's swift eclipse,
   Fruition, life unzoned of death, must rise, —
Its dawning mount to vast apocalypse,
   Evolving vaster immortalities.

GO NOT AWAY.

GO not away, Lord! Leave us not
     Amid the mystery of out lot,
Life's baffling problem half unwrought—
Nor haunting doubt, nor halting thought,
Can work the far solution out;
Thy love alone can make it plain—
Why high resolve in us is slain,
Why dear to us the tempter's call,
And why we falter till we fall,
Thou who rememberest we are dust,
Who gave our little day in trust,
Knoweth the meaning of it all.

Go not away!   We travel on;
And every hour that rest is won,
We feel we need Thy love anew, —
To save us from the deed we'd do,
To strengthen for the deed undone;
To help the aching feet to run
With patience all the tiresome road;
To lighten some the weary load
That every life must bear alone,
Save Thou dost make its weight Thine own.
Thy ministering angels still are sent
To cheer us in our banishment;
Their sinless hands, extended fair,
Lighten our sense of human care;
They lend us life all unaware,
Show where its deep fruitions are;
They bring Thee near in dear reward, —
Go not away belovèd Lord!

When sinking low the sordid day
Shuts spiritual things away,
And dimmer grows our seeking sight,
Weaker our reaching after right;

Then, if our faintest purpose flower
To perfect deed, its perfect hour
Hath birth in *Thee.* All-fusing Power!
That stirs the music in the reed,
The plaint in the imprisoned tree,
The bliss in golden belted bee;
That wafts the insect on its wing
That works the miracle of Spring,
And in Thy secret place doth nurse
The forces of Thy Universe;
Oh, how much more wilt Thou sustain
The souls that in Thy likeness reign!

When dawns the hour of supreme pain,
When life itself through love be slain
And we live dead, — the spirit's cry
Is all for Thee, O Love unseen,
To fill the need that hath not been
By any human passion filled,
By any human giving stilled;
For Thee — for only Thee — its cry,
O Love Supreme, to satisfy!

Thus when some morning dawneth gray
Above a desolated day,
And low we murmur: "Why arise?
There is no work beneath the skies
That's worth the doing, — nor a joy
That does not beckon to destroy;"
We sink beneath life's utmost cross,
The aching sense of utter loss,
The silent house, the empty chair,
The death-void mocking grief's despair.

In our last struggle dread and deep,
That meets us ere the rounding sleep;
When deeps of Being strive with deep,
All life for life, all life with death,
And we yield up our mortal breath
To what?   In this world's swift eclipse,
Grant us the last apocalypse
Of final vision.   Let us see
The life of life that makes us free,
The sum of being ours to be,
The sum of loving, seeing Thee.

A LITANY.

SHOW to me Thy tender favor:
  Spite of all my sad behavior,
Well I love Thee, O my Saviour!

Well I love Thee; on Thee leaning
I do comprehend love's meaning:
Thy love, me from world-love weaning.

Pouring treasure all unheeded,
Giving all where none is needed,
Well for me Thou interceded.

All my soul's fine incense wasted,
All life's sweet and bitter tasted,
Slow to Thee my hurt heart hasted.

Spare the cup of retribution,
Save me from all sin's pollution,
Give me Thy love's absolution.

By the grandeur of Thy teaching;
By Thy mercy, all need reaching;
By Thy last cry's sad beseeching;

By Thy prayer " Forgive " still sounding
Down the ages, men confounding;
By Thine own love's cruel wounding, —

Take the love, the all, I 'm owing,
Take my being's overflowing,
Lest it wander in its going.

A CONVERSATION.

A LOVELIER than Italian sun
    Went down this eve when day was
      done;
'T was then a dear voice said to me:
"Why you fear death I cannot see.

"To me the way looks straight and plain,
From dark to light, from loss to gain:
Each night I lay my burden down,
Tired of my cross, I ask my crown.

"And so I pray to-morrow's sun
May rise to see my journey done,
Progression's endless race begun;
The utmost meed of being won.

"But you, with all your griefs and tears,
How close you clasp the fleeting years;
You never sigh, in weal or woe,
For sweeter life than this you know."

I answered: "Truth you tell, dear friend,
Along the earth my footsteps tend;
The grave looks cold and lonesome; I
Say often, 'Oh, how sad to die!'

"Forever more the mocking skies'
Illimitable mysteries
Foretell the being yet to be;
Yet all it is I cannot see.

"I am so human, how forego
This life for life I cannot know?
Can seraph sympathy above
Be more than this our mortal love?

"We humbly lean upon his Word,
And deem at last we love the Lord;
Yet we, whene'er our poor hearts bleed,
Cling to each other in our need.

"Than thee I need no tenderer friend
To walk with to my journey's end;
The pathway might be smooth or rough,
This crowning joy would be enough.

"I gaze beyond the faintest star,
And say: 'My Father, thou art far!'
No voice comes down the solemn sphere
To say: 'Dear child, thy Friend is near.'

"I never saw my Saviour's face,
Nor felt His healing touch of grace;
And far and dim they seem to be,
Those walks beside the Galilee.

"In sooth, in vain I try to paint
The ecstasy of soaring saint,
Whose faith, through all the dimming mist,
His garments here hath reached and kissed.

"Not so I see!   My clouded eyes
Look longing up the soundless skies;
Yet, veering near to subtler sense,
Comes no star-eyed Intelligence.

"And yet, some day, some light must fall
At least from off the outer wall;
When you go in the Wondrous Gate,
A ray may reach me ere too late.

"If not a single shadow lies
Upon your soul's unclouded skies,
Far better you should go some day,
And then come back to show the way.

"Though all my light of life had fled,
I should not be disquieted,
Nor fear, although I could not see,
If you would reach your hand to me.

"Ah, then, though faltering, fearing much,
At thrill of that belovèd touch,
Would die the cruel, darkening doubt —
No mystery be past finding out.

"The death-stream might be swift and wide,
In peace I'd gain the thither side;
Though deep and dark and dread its flow,
I should not be afraid to go."

At last the primrose splendor fled;
And twilight purple stained instead
The sunset gates, the silent skies,
That shut from sight our Paradise.

" So darkly dim the distant gleam,
My Love," I said, " it is a dream.
I see, within your bending eyes,
The living light that never dies;
This deathless love within the soul
Is prophet of its perfect goal."

THE CHRIST.

THOU livest on the earth, dear Lord!
   Thou art not far away,
A name within a misty word, —
   Thou 'rt with us here to-day.

We 've listened to the battle's shock,
   The weary cry of creeds:
Unmoved the Shepherd of His flock
   His loving people leads.

Thou livest on the earth, dear Lord!
   What tears of sorrow flow,
What toil there is, what poor reward,
   What want Thy children know!

Thou livest on the earth to-day
  Wherever Patience stands,
Where holy Love kneels down to pray,
  Where Faith uplifts her hands.

And thus, alike in storm or shine,
  We lift our eyes to see
Thy lovely face, Thy face divine,
  Thy face that makes us free, —

Free from the shadow sin has cast,
  Free from all passions ill,
And free to rest, when life is past,
  In regions fair and still.

So fearing much, and loving much,
  The tides of life we stem,
And stretch a faltering hand to touch
  Thy far-off garment's hem, —

That haply to our souls at length
  Thy saving grace may flow,
And we may gain the wingèd strength
  Thy ransomed children know.

So halting, falling often, in
　The kingdom of our birth:
What joy, — our Heavenly kinsman still
　Walks with us on earth.

PRAY THOU FOR ME.

TO ——.

PRAY thou for me.   The way is dark,
    The star of Faith I scarcely see;
It lights for thee Heaven's loftiest arc, —
    Pray thou for me.

I stand mid human battle hot,
    The war of men is strange to see;
But then I never chose my lot, —
    Pray thou for me.

Pray thou for me.   Close is thy grasp
    Upon the things that are unseen;
The Cross of Christ I see thee clasp,
    And on it lean.

Pray thou for me.   His nameless grace,
 His life of life, mine eyes would see;
The love that lights my Saviour's face
  May fall on me.

Pray thou for me.   The common air
 Will stronger, purer seem to be,
And all the world will grow more fair, —
  Pray thou for me.

Pray thou for me.   Before my sight
 Will spread horizons vast and clear;
Rays from the highest heaven will light
  My heaven here.

THE MESSAGE.

I WAITED, waited; all the days were long,
    And even joy hinted of weary dearth;
A longed-for note I missed from every song.
    "The finest good is never found on earth,"
I said; "E'en beauty's self is touched by wrong."

The years were long. I waited. Lo! no voice
    Smote the high keynote I so yearned to hear;
No word of power made my soul rejoice
    In sacred faith untouched of human fear,
    No word immortal brought all heaven near.

The upper ether of divinest truth
    I had not mounted to. I could not gain
Its shining summit by the road of ruth,
    Its perfect peace by mortal loss and pain:
    The years were long, and faith in me was slain.

So scarce I listened when the Autumn air
   Bore in a voice.   It cried: " Believe, believe !
How poor the cloak of doubt thy soul doth wear !
   How low the life that leads thee on to grieve !
   Only they live, who, claiming faith, believe.

" Believe, tried heart, the Lord doth love his own.
   Inalienable, ever, He doth hold
Its home of homes for every spirit lone,
   Wherein the Love Supreme shall yet enfold
Each orphaned soul that here doth make its moan."

   .   .   .   .   .

Lo! I believe.   No day is ever long,
   No life-task tiresome in my happy hand.
A deeper note trembles within my song:
   Some way the listening angels understand,
The while I sing, the heart in me grows strong.

Dear tiny trust!   With what a tender care
   I love and nourish thee this mortal hour;
Sure, further on, from Thee, supernal, fair,
   I 'll see evolve Faith's full, consummate flower,
Mine own, dear Lord, before Thy face to wear.

SONNETS.

SONNETS.

———•◦•———

TO RALPH WALDO EMERSON.

O MY great master!   As the swift years fly,
   And we fly with them, here I make this sign.
I set thy name with things I deem divine,
That one day, haply, thou, in passing by,
May chance to see it, burning lone and high,
   And know it thine.   O spirit, pure and fine,
   Let thy deep inner vision read the line,
And read the soul that writes it falteringly.

Thy hopeless debtor, I; the debt, how grand.
   Lo! I do hasten, lest it be too late,
To lay a flower in thy kindly hand;
The while I point thee to the farther sky,
   Where glows thy name, beyond all fleeting fate,
White, shining in its own eternity.

TO JOHN GREENLEAF WHITTIER.

I.

DEAR singer, gentle teacher, grave and grand,
　　Yet tender always, as thou 'rt true and wise,
　I must believe thy softly serious eyes
The unseen doth divine, doth understand.
Two angels,* holding memory's mystic band,
　　Discernest thou, in yon mysterious skies?
　　Their sweet, lost presence all about thee lies,
As when, in life, they took thee by the hand.

All light was one; she waved Wit's airy wand,
　　Moved all to laughter, lavished Humor's wine.
Her sumptuous spirit, tropic breezes fanned.
　　　In Alice' gentler eyes, Grief unconfest
　　　Bewept her lost; but I did love her best,
　While Phœbe poured for thee the draught divine.

* Alice and Phœbe Cary.

II.

In my fair youth I loved thy household lay, —
· Thy song of love more than thy fiery strain.
Its haunting sweetness, tender unto pain,
Deep from the heart of that enchanting May,
Doth pierce the splendor of my high noonday.
Its low, long murmur trembles in my brain,
Till all its purples youth puts on again,
And flushed of dawn Love's first auroras play.

Lo! as I listen, through the Summer balm
I hear a later song, a song of rest;
No morning carol, — 't is a twilight psalm,
The soul's prophetic pæan. Mounting, blest,
It bears aloft the saint's triumphant calm.
Dear heart! thine after-song I love the best.

APHRODITE URANIA.

FAIR child of Uranus! O heavenly one!
   They sin who do thy holy self profane —
  Who, in the name of Love, do set a stain
Upon thy robes of sheer sea-splendor spun,
Upon thy worship sacred as the sun.
   When Eros met thee by the mighty main,
   When Graces decked thee on Cythera's plain,
Goddess of Heaven, love first on earth begun.

O Aphrodite, fair Dodona's dove
   Is thy white symbol. Piteous 't is that blame
Should fall on thee, from Libitina's love, —
   She so unworthy thy high crown to claim.
Alas, to-day one single soul should rove
   To her, to sin, all in thy sacred name!

HERA.

DEEP-BOSOMED Hera, sumptuous mother
    fair, —
  Thou prov'st to woman, spite her adverse fate,
  The utmost grandeur of her high estate,
By the Hellenic crown thy brow doth wear.
Empress of Home — of Heaven's supernal air,
  Comrade of Zeus, his dear and sacred mate,
  Sovereign of woman, be she low or great!
So let all womanhood thy splendor bear

In joy, that outward from Time's nebulous morn
  Doth shine, refulgent, on this later day,
Of elemental attributes unshorn,
  A goddess-woman, formed for lofty sway, —
Yet one, no less for love and beauty born,
  In wifely state shedding her farthest ray.

PALLAS ATHENA.

O MIGHTY Pallas! Woman-god supreme,
 Kindler of purpose, not of weak desire,
 Thine emblem, ether, full of light and fire.
The Athenian woman, held in dis-esteem,
Beheld in thee, fulfilled, her hopeless dream;
 Knowledge, to her, was infamy entire.
 Yet thou, a goddess, heroes didst inspire, —
Thine Ægis power, brightened by Honor's beam.

Athena Parthenos! How long the pain!
 How long the shame! Thy golden voice was
  dumb;
And men were selfish, slow high truth to praise.
 But lo! at last thy large-browed daughters come,
Their lovely eyelids shedding Wisdom's rays;
 In Reason's radiant realm with thee they reign.

A MAGNOLIA GRANDIFLORA.*

HALF flame, half fragrance, wonderful thou art,
   O peerless blossom! Fold on fold of snow,
  Swathing from careless eyes its inner glow,
Doth lie, unsullied, on thy golden heart.
World-voices harsh roll inward from the mart,
   The rude winds idly through thy petals flow,
   And dusts of highways on thy beauty blow;
But, pure as ether, thou dost bloom apart.

How like thy giver art thou, regnant flower!
   Thy stainless stole, like hers, doth starlike shine;
Thy folded samite is her rich heart's dower.
   Thy mystic cup, thy consecrated wine,
All symbolize her spiritual power,
   Regina, reigning by Love's holiest shrine.

* The last Magnolia that bloomed for Mrs. Hayes in the White
House, 1881.

FRUITAGE.

I SEE the heavy-fruited days go by.
   " To-morrow, fair to-morrow, thou wilt bring
  The chance I want to pluck the sweetest thing,
The highest apple on the bough," I cry.
Bearing rich treasure fleet, they fly, they fly,
   Full-freighted days, with no returning wing,
   Till winnowed Winter's shadows climb and cling,
And emptied boughs wave under barren sky.

Your charm all lingers in my heart's recall,
  O days so royal — rich in bounty blest!
On want ye woke your largess sure would fall;
  Hungry, unfed, ye left me like the rest, —
The fruit I could not reach, sweetest of all,
  Still taunts my spirit at its stinted feast.

INADEQUACY.

I SAW a fallen swallow on the street
   Beat on the cruel stone its wounded wing,
   And lift its voiceful throat as if to sing.
It sought to soar, as if on pinion fleet;
It stirred with inchoate song, so sweet, so sweet,
   That died unsung.   The poor, low murmuring,
   Wrung of its pain, how pitiful a thing,
While mocked the Heaven it could not rise to meet!

Ah! thus we greet the challenge of the sky;
   The far fulfilment we can never gain,
   For wounding circumstance and wilting pain
Hold back the soaring soul that fain would fly.
   We seek to sing the high immortal strain;
But close to earth flutters our futile cry.

FATE.

I COULD but love thee, when I saw thy face, —
   The dear fulfilment of Life's loveliest years.
  Through toil and sorrow, change, and many tears,
How long I 'd waited for its nameless grace!
It rose above me in its lofty place;
   Beyond my hope, beyond its haunting fears,
   I knew thee, loved thee. But our kindred spheres
Shivered and parted in dividing space.

I can but love thee. Though from heights afar,
   In mystic aureole, as from distant skies,
Remote as incommunicable star,
   Still strikes the summons of thy dominant eyes,
   To smite my sundered spirit, while it cries
For thee, forever dear as thou art far.

RENUNCIATION.

HERE on Thy sacred altar, dear God, see,
    I lay the priceless treasure of my soul, —
The love I poured with such unstinted dole,
The poorest thing it touched seemed rich to me.
Take it, O Lord! I give it all to Thee!
    Take it and shut it in Thy heavenly goal,
    Where Life's fair fantasy hath no control,
Where lonely human need can never be.

I turn and leave it — never any more
    To be my comrade, dearer in its thrall
Than all companions. On far sea or shore
    I never lost the sweetness of its call;
It won me from all loves I loved before.
    I give it Thee, and so my soul gives all.

OPULENCE.

THOU art too rich, though not in hoarded gold;
    Beyond all hunger of thy daily need,
  Hath human approbation's honeyed meed
In lavish word and act on thee been rolled.
Too oft hath tell-tale heart its story told
    Of lonely love that straight to thee did lead
    In wistful ministry, in pleading deed;
Self-centred, high, it found thee only cold.

Thou art too rich!   Had grief, a soundless sea,
    Deluged thy life till not one hope were left;
Hadst thou missed love, fulfilment manifold —
    Thy life all want, or hopelessly bereft —
Scornful of gifts one poor would die to hold,
Thou couldst not walk this earth so proud and free.

SECRETIVENESS.

How dear thy secret, past all guile or art,
　　The sacred secret of thy morning day!
　It rules thy soul with most inviolate sway;
It holds thee from man's common lot apart—
A king amid the multitudinous mart,
　　Invincible forever in the fray.
　　What mounting hosts thy citadel essay,
Thy mailèd lip, thine unsurrendering heart.

They peer where Motive's pulses beat and glow,
　　Where Love's embalmed that living made thee
　　　　blest,
Where Memory from thy past doth still bestow
　The dearest thing thy sumptuous youth possest.
In vain, in vain!　Thou wilt not yielding show
　The guarded treasure of thy bolted breast.

DISTANCE.

HOW many leagues of weary land and sea
　　Can place thy spirit far apart from mine?
　Can lure from distance dim some silent sign
To set my soul enfranchised far from thee, —
Afar from eyes that never leave me free,
　　From tones that stir my heart like mounting wine,
　　From Presence thralling as some dream divine?
Alas! by night and day all stay with me.

There is no distance, — not for those who know
　The silent countersign that makes them one,
Whose thoughts are messengers that burn and glow,
　With Love's fleet messages the winds outrun.
　Go, sail the seas! Go, seek the rising sun!
Beyond my constant heart thou canst not go.

RECOGNITION.

HOW hast thou overtaken me midway,
　　Thou young athlete?　It is high noon with me,
　While still on thy ascending pathway, see
The unbrushed dews.　Thine eyes are full of May;
Above thy cloudless brows the aureoles play
　　Of early morning.　Fate I cannot flee;
　Arid and bare my road runs drearily.
Why beside mine do thy feet lingering stray?

Am I so weary?　In the shadeless noon
　　My heart yearns only for a sheltered seat,
Folded in silence like a grassy dune,
Folded in fragrance like a rose in June,
　　Where two may find communion full and sweet;
And thou, thou only, learned my heart so soon.

THE FRIEND.

BE thou my friend. I want no lover now;
    For love, man's love, is selfish overmuch.
The dear caress, the glance, the tone, the touch,
The all in all he claims in overflow,
Or standeth injured. All the friend's deep glow
    Is for his friend; and in the rack and rush
    We call the world, nothing I need, as such
A friend. Thy faithful hand's swift blow

Beats back the world, — its questioning doubt.
    What balsam to my heart thy faith doth yield!
Lo! in my friend I bide, on him I lean,
    As one assaulted, on a steadfast shield.
No dread attack can put my trust to rout;
The past is all as if it had not been.

THE LOVER.

NAY, I will be thy Lover, thou my Love!
    Here now I swear thee fealty, dear one,
  While all my days do seek thee as the sun!
Thy Lover first is friend, that he may prove
That he is worthy thee, all men above.
    To largess of all joy I proudly run;
    The royal race of comradeship begun,
Ends fast in love that cannot fail or rove.

This is my joy, to serve thee, — to exalt
    Thy name, to call thee Queen of all thy kind;
Sovereign of life and love to me thou art.
    I marry thy rich melodies of mind;
I see thee large and fair without a fault.
Take thou thy throne, O Empress of my heart!

FULFILMENT.

WHAT did I do with all the years at best
    Before I knew thee? Did no mystic chord
  Tremble with prescience of the crowning word
At last to make my life divinely blest?
What could I find in all my eager quest
    Of dreamed-of joy, of labor's slow reward,
    When I had never seen my sole Life's Lord,
Nor ever entered into Love's large rest?

Ah! now I know why fair young days were dark,
    Why piteous tears of youth fell swiftly down,
Why at the dawning sang no morning lark,
    Why sullen afternoons were full of frown.
I had not reached thy being's larger arc,
    Nor worn, as thy great gift, Love's sacred crown.

THE CATHEDRAL PINES.*

I.

AFAR, mid pictured saints and symboled signs,
  Through great cathedral arches warm and
    dim,
  I caught the melody of matin hymn;
Susurrous still it thrills these resonant lines,
The morning symphony of soaring pines,
  Whose flowering columns, springing straight and
    slim,
  Deep prick with emerald Aurora's rim,
While Prayer and Praise below do build their
    shrines.

Melodious minster of enchanting health,
  What worship murmurs in thine undertone!
  What healing hides in every honeyed cone, —
Balsamic life sweet breathing out by stealth.
  What gifts to mortals, on thy breezes blown,
Bring balm to flesh and spirit in thy wealth!

* At Intervale, North Conway, N. H.

ABOVE, the azure's plenitude of space;
   Below, in shady wood-aisle's sacred hush,
   The holy hymn sweet sung by hermit thrush.
No longer hidden in the secret place,
Jehovah smiles through all the Summer's grace;
   He draweth near in sunset's kindling flush,
   He speaks to me from Nature's blazing bush.
Lo! close I see Thee, Father, face to face!

Unscared the feeblest creature hears Thy call;
   In slanting sunbeam swims the happy mote;
   The idle flies in ample ether float;
Safe on the mossy floor small bird-feet fall;
   Thou must not miss Thy larger creature's note,
She sees Thee, sings Thee, loves Thee all in all.

THE JOY OF WORK.

THE promise of delicious youth may fail;
　　The fair fulfilment of our Summer-time
May wane and wither at its hour of prime;
The gorgeous glow of Hope may swiftly pale;
E'en Love may leave us spite our piteous wail;
　　The heart, defeated, desolate may climb
　　To lonely Reason on her height sublime;
Bnt one sure fort no foe can e'er assail.

'T is thine, O Work, — the joy supreme of thought,
　　Where feeling, purpose, and long patience meet;
Where in deep silence the ideal wrought
　　Bourgeons from blossoming to fruit complete.
O crowning bliss!　O treasure never bought!
　　All else may perish, thou remainest sweet.

University Press: John Wilson and Son, Cambridge.

www.ingramcontent.com/pod-product-compliance
Lightning Source LLC
Chambersburg PA
CBHW020338030726
47496CB00007B/1938